D1053397

THE
SCENT OF
BURNT
FLOWERS

THE
SCENT OF
BURNT
FLOWERS

A NOVEL

BLITZ BAZAWULE

BALLANTINE BOOKS

NEW YORK

Copyright © 2022 by Blitz Baza, Inc.

Published in the United States by Ballantine Books, an imprint of Random House, a division of Penguin Random House LLC, New York.

BALLANTINE and the HOUSE colophon are registered trademarks of Penguin Random House LLC.

LIBRARY OF CONGRESS CATALOGING-IN-PUBLICATION DATA
Names: Bazawule, Blitz, author.
Title: The scent of burnt flowers : a novel / Blitz Bazawule.
Description: New York : Ballantine Books, [2022]
Identifiers: LCCN 2021054440 (print) | LCCN 2021054441 (ebook) |
ISBN 9780593496237 (hardcover) | ISBN 9780593496244 (ebook)
Subjects: LCSH: African American couples—Fiction. | Fugitives from justice—
Fiction. | Ghana—History—Coup d'état, 1966—Fiction. | LCGFT:
Magic realist fiction. | Historical fiction. | Novels.
Classification: LCC PS3602.A9935 S27 2022 (print) |
LCC PS3602.A9935 (ebook) | DDC 813/.6—dc23/eng/20211124
LC record available at https://lccn.loc.gov/2021054440
LC ebook record available at https://lccn.loc.gov/2021054441

Printed in Canada on acid-free paper

randomhousebooks.com

2 4 6 8 9 7 5 3 1

First Edition

Book design by Victoria Wong

For Jai

"Aboa bi beka wo a, ne ofiri wo ntoma mu."
AKAN PROVERB

"If an animal will bite you, it will be
from your cloth."

PART 1

CHAPTER 1

Accra, 1966

B ernadette awoke to the sound of a loud blast and thought Melvin had shot himself. She had feared this day would come, yet nothing could prepare her for it. The flickering light that illuminated the small hotel room blinded her as she slid off the bed trembling. She could feel her heart pounding through the silk nightgown she had hurriedly packed the night they fled Philadelphia for Accra, a city she had only read about in the newspapers.

The story was about a young boxer who won a gold medal at the 1964 Olympic games. "Accra," she had said out loud, finding the name fascinating. She never imagined that she would be a fugitive in that same city just two years later.

The sound of gunfire piercing the air jolted Bernadette once more. The hotel balcony door swung open, sending in a rush of light. Melvin leaned in and smiled. "It's just fireworks, babe. Happy New Year!" She sighed, deeply relieved. The sky burst into a thousand shimmering colors silhouetting Melvin's towering frame. Even then, she could still see his bright piercing eyes, gazing ardently at her. Bernadette wrapped her arms around his broad shoulders and sobbed quietly.

"It'll all work out, babe, I promise," Melvin whispered.

This wasn't the first time Bernadette had heard those words, but tonight she believed him. Maybe it was the cacophonous crowds celebrating the new year or the ephemeral fireflies floating through the night sky. She truly believed it would all work out. Melvin poured Bernadette a glass of water and they sat on the hotel balcony watching the fishermen stagger in a drunken stupor. A crackling bonfire brightened the canoe sails that billowed at the mercy of the wind, casting an ominous shadow on the beach. Occasionally, a young couple or two would stroll hand in hand toward the crashing waves, avoiding the large groups of women clad in all white who had congregated for a new year's prayer meeting. Amid the pulsating atmosphere, a somber highlife tune seeped out of a nearby transistor radio, captivating Melvin and Bernadette. Melvin held his hand out to her, a small assurance. They swayed in each other's arms, overlooking the glimmering fireworks that brightened the city that had given them temporary refuge. Bernadette felt the ocean breeze and mosquitoes buzzing around her ear, and she thought about how similar Accra was to her childhood home of Baton Rouge, Louisiana. The humid smell that lingered after a brief downpour reminded Bernadette of a story her grandmother told her about the day she was born. A day she thought about more frequently as she worried her days were drawing nigh.

IT WAS THE summer of 1935, and a season of hurricanes and heavy rains had flooded the Mississippi River. Bernadette's mother, Alice Broussard, was already in labor when news of the broken levees spread like wildfire. Bernadette's father, Bernard Broussard, had died earlier that summer in a bizarre boat accident on the same Mississippi River that would soon swallow Baton Rouge. The only family Alice had was Bernadette's grandmother, Ma' Susan. The two lived in a small shotgun house near Magnolia Mound Plantation, an edifice that conjured the enduring legacy of chattel slavery. The flood soon overwhelmed everything south of Merrydale, and the ineptitude of the state relief agency guaranteed a muddled rescue effort.

When it finally began, the evacuation was for white residents only. Alice and Ma' Susan hid in the attic, hoping the top floor would serve as safety, but they were soon submerged. The ferocious thunderstorm that battered the house that night drowned Alice's screams as she pushed new life into the world. Ma' Susan held her breath underwater long enough to cut the umbilical cord and wrap baby Bernadette in a wet blanket. That was when she witnessed a moment so magical that she never told anyone, except Bernadette.

Alice began to drift below the attic, which had mysteriously collapsed into a vast ocean. An otherworldly light emanated from her torso, transforming her into a mermaid. As Ma' Susan struggled to keep Bernadette afloat, a force lifted them above the water. Alice smiled, waved, and disappeared into the deep dark ocean, leaving Ma' Susan forlorn and grief-stricken. Her tears were swallowed by the deluge, which had now reached the ceiling. Then Wilbert Benoit, a beloved Negro businessman, floated to the attic window with his paddleboat. He had been circling West McKinley Street searching for survivors when he heard the wailing cries of a baby. It took almost an hour of prying and sawing to bring baby Bernadette and Ma' Susan safely aboard.

The subsequent scale of destruction was overwhelming. It

took six months of dredging for the floodwater to recede. When it finally did, Alice's body was never found. Ma' Susan remained unequivocal about what she had witnessed that night. She called Bernadette "Water Baby" and often recounted her mythical birth story.

Of course, Bernadette didn't believe a word of it, but her affinity for water was evident nonetheless. She spent countless hours in the beige clawfoot bathtub her grandmother had bought at a yard sale. Bernadette often passed out while submerged. On more than one occasion her grandmother walked in and thought she had drowned. It seemed Bernadette could breathe underwater as easily as she did above it. Now, with her present predicament, she wished for that same ease of breath.

A GENTLE TUG on Bernadette's shoulder woke her up. She turned to see Melvin fully dressed and lighting a cigarette nervously. "We gotta go, babe," he stammered.

Bernadette sprang to her feet. "They found us?"

"Not sure, but it's best we go now."

Flustered, Bernadette dashed into the hotel room, leaving Melvin to languish on the balcony. He took an anxious drag, exhaled, and cast his gaze across the street, where the fishermen had celebrated the new year. The first light of sunrise blinded him. Abrasive sounds of cars honking and haggling street vendors added to his throbbing headache. Accra was indeed a sprawling metropolis, and from where Melvin stood, he could see it all. The stoic police officer in his crisp colonial uniform, overwhelmed by the traffic. Motorcycles and rickshaws, zigzagging past frustrated passengers in boneshaker buses. European businessmen ill-adjusted to the tropical heat.

And in the middle of it all stood the statue of the man who had brought independence. The reason Melvin and Bernadette had fled to Ghana in the first place—Kwame Nkrumah.

"I'M READY," BERNADETTE said as she stepped onto the balcony wearing a colorful floral dress. She adjusted her wide-brimmed hat that rendered her inconspicuous. Her smooth brown skin glowed in the humid equatorial heat, as she dabbed beads of sweat trickling down her forehead. Bernadette had celebrated her thirty-first birthday earlier that year, but her youthful features inherited from her great-grandmother said otherwise. Those same features were the reason Bernadette could never pass as a local. Her high cheekbones, narrow slanted eyes, and statuesque figure were enough to label her *obroni,* a term that was originally used for European colonists but had morphed to mean foreigners of all races. To avoid standing out too much, Bernadette had planned to braid her long curly hair before they left Philadelphia, but under the circumstances a simple ponytail would suffice. Melvin tossed his half-smoked cigarette and crushed it under the heel of his shoe.

"How many of them you see?" Bernadette asked, grabbing her suitcase.

"Two, maybe three. If they ain't FBI, they sure dress like 'em," Melvin said, adjusting his pastor's collar in the mirror. The same pastor's collar he had bought at the Snyder Avenue Costume Shop in Philadelphia. The Christian missionary disguise was the best option he could find. To Melvin's surprise, he actually looked the part. His dark shaven face, precisely parted hair, and general fastidiousness gave him the air of a clergyman. Melvin had just turned forty-two and his Sidney

Poitier–esque posture made his costume fit like it was tailored. Bernadette was supposed to play the pastor's wife, even though they were only engaged. Melvin flipped the suitcase buckle and grabbed a .38-caliber Ruger. He tucked it in the small of his back and recalled how simple it was to smuggle a loaded gun on an international flight. As long as the customs officers saw his Bible and pastor's collar, he was exempt from all scrutiny. It also helped that all the men were distracted by Bernadette's perfect hourglass figure, a sticky point for Melvin in their otherwise stable relationship.

A knock on the door startled Melvin and Bernadette. They exchanged nervous looks as the knock echoed again. Melvin dug out the revolver and aimed it steadily at the door.

"Who is it?"

"Cleaning, sah," a languid voice replied.

Bernadette sank into the bed, relieved. Melvin lowered the revolver. "No cleaning today, ma'am."

They waited until they heard the cleaning lady wheel her cart to the next room, then grabbed their bags and snuck out through the hotel balcony. Melvin and Bernadette hurried down a spiral staircase that wrapped around a large neon sign that read *SEA VIEW HOTEL.*

The diagonal arches led to the hotel lobby, where Melvin had gotten in the habit of scouring through local Ghanaian newspapers. He feigned curiosity about local news, but his real objective was to make sure there was no mention of either him or Bernadette. That was where he struck up a conversation with the front desk receptionist about Cape Coast.

She was a tall woman with tight braids that appeared to pull her large eyes farther apart.

"Yes sah, Cape Coast is where most of our guests go for

sightseeing," she told Melvin in an affable tone. "It's not too busy as Accra and the beaches are cleaner." She scribbled a list of accommodations and sightseeing options on a hotel pad, then told him where he could catch the bus.

As MELVIN AND Bernadette approached the bus station, a group of head porters jostled to offer their services.

"Pastor, make I carry give you," they muttered in a chorus.

"Pastor wife, I beg make I carry." They turned their attention to Bernadette when they realized Melvin was unyielding.

He had been warned by the same receptionist never to let go of their bags, especially the one that hung on his shoulder where he carried all his money. So Melvin declined the head porters, much to their chagrin. They meandered through a queue of passengers engulfed in billowing smoke from a vendor selling roasted bush meat. A repugnant air hung over the bus station. A rare blend of sweat, frustration, and indifference. Bernadette kept her white handkerchief blocking her nasal passages, breathing only through her mouth. The occasional hurling of insults between a group of bus drivers punctuated the riotous passengers.

Melvin finally spotted the ticket counter, a makeshift stall that hadn't seen a coat of paint in years. The man sitting behind it was a sort of relic himself. His faded oversized cap, a hand-me-down from a former British administrator, covered his deep sunken eyes.

He lifted it when he asked, "Where to, sah?"

"Cape Coast," Melvin answered, digging in his wallet.

The ticket agent pointed ahead. "You want coach, boneshaker, or bus?"

The coaches had been imported by the British colonial

government. Although they were more luxurious, they took twice the amount of time to get to their destination. The bone-shakers were used to transport farm produce and the few passengers brave enough to share close quarters with goats, chickens, and sometimes wild boars.

"We'll take the bus, please," Bernadette said.

The ticket agent nodded and ripped out two tickets. "Good choice."

The aroma of roasted plantain and groundnuts filled the bus as Melvin and Bernadette climbed aboard. Bernadette slid into the window seat, fanning herself vigorously. Her efforts only exacerbated Accra's sweltering heat, which she was beginning to detest. A young vendor approached Bernadette's window carrying a stack of freshly baked bread that seemed to reach the heavens. She mumbled something in a local dialect, and Bernadette shook her head. "My dear, I don't understand."

A woman wearing a large headscarf turned to Bernadette. "She said she likes your hat."

Bernadette thanked her and bought a loaf of bread she didn't intend to eat. The passengers jolted forward as the driver put the bus in motion. Loosely welded seats squeaked with each pothole they encountered, competing with the fluttering sound of the diesel engine that left a pungent smell in the bus. To make things worse, a discordant highlife song blared out the janky speakers as the bus sped down the dusty road.

MELVIN'S HEADACHE HAD subsided when the bus passed a sign reading *YOU ARE LEAVING ACCRA REGION.* Bernadette was fast asleep, slumped over her seat. Melvin glanced at the empty road and it made him nostalgic. He pulled out an old photograph from his wallet and rubbed his thumb across the worn edges. The feeling transported him as he gazed at himself, twenty-five years younger, standing next to his then best friend and now president of Ghana, Kwame Nkrumah.

How Melvin and Nkrumah met on the front steps of Lincoln University was a case of serendipity. Melvin had never dreamt of going to college. In fact, no one in his family had ever made it past the sixth grade. It was expected that Melvin would join his father at Mr. Moretti's sawmill, which had already employed two generations of Johnsons. Melvin's grandfather, Otis Johnson, had worked at the sawmill after he saved enough money to purchase his wife's and son's freedom from a Virginia plantation. Otis was a master saw operator and soon trained his son, Earl, as his assistant. Melvin was next in line, or at least he thought so, until the day of the accident. Everyone knew his father was an alcoholic, but it never affected his work. He must have been inebriated beyond what was usual, because one afternoon, he ran the saw without lumber. When the metal blade started shooting sparks, Earl stuck his hand inside to stop it. Needless to say, it was a bloody mess when the ambulance finally arrived. As Melvin stared at his father's bloody tourniquet and heard the sirens wailing down the road, he made up his mind right then, anything was better than Mr. Moretti's sawmill.

That summer, Melvin applied to Lincoln University after discovering that his favorite poet, Langston Hughes, was an alumnus. He had very little hope of being accepted, however. So when the letter came in a white paper envelope, it took him a whole week to open it. When he finally did, he found a full-ride scholarship and a bus ticket from Virginia to Pennsylvania.

Melvin's father didn't say goodbye on the day he departed for Lincoln University. He just stared at him through the window and took a swig from his whiskey flask with his good arm. Melvin's mother, however, accompanied him to the bus depot. As she hugged him, she whispered, "Your daddy loves you, he just scared for you is all."

The early September cold pierced through Melvin's frayed polyester coat as he climbed into the Greyhound bus. He made his way to the cramped colored section, eyeing the empty seats reserved for whites only. A nervous feeling swept through Melvin, although he was glad to be escaping the draconian social order below the Mason-Dixon.

After eight uncomfortable hours, the bus pulled into Lincoln University's parking lot. Melvin alighted, dragging his suitcase behind him. His posture loosened as he gazed at the mammoth campus. Then a voice startled him. "You are new here too?" Melvin turned sharply to see a set of curious eyes staring back at him through round glasses.

"Nkrumah—my name is Nkrumah," the stranger said, shaking Melvin's hand vigorously.

Melvin couldn't place the accent, but it reminded him of a Liberian fella he once met at Mr. Moretti's sawmill. "Melvin Johnson, my friends call me Mel."

They walked through the campus gate as Nkrumah fidgeted with his oversized suit.

"I'm from the Gold Coast."

"Gold Coast? Where's that?"

"West Africa, below the Upper Volta."

"Ah, I see. I'm from Virginia," Melvin said, trying to keep up with Nkrumah's brisk pace. They joined a stream of freshmen rummaging through a list of names and dormitories. After a brief search, Melvin turned to Nkrumah. "I'm in Amos Hall, you?"

Nkrumah squinted, adjusted his glasses, and smiled. "I am in Amos Hall too."

A LOUD BELL summoned the freshman students to the chapel that stood on the northern end of campus. Melvin gazed at the bright beams of light shooting through the stained-glass windows. They illuminated the ornate arches and long wooden pews. The murmuring chatter of students was interrupted by a thundering baritone voice.

"I want to welcome our freshman class to Lincoln University. My name is Reverend Walter Brooks. I'm a proud alumnus of this mighty institution, the first of its kind founded in North America." He dabbed his forehead with a moist handkerchief and nodded at a group of white men seated capriciously behind him.

"For more than eighty years, Lincoln University has been training leaders to work among the Negro race, and to serve the cause of better relations between the races." He paused for applause and continued. "It gives me great pleasure to introduce our president, Walter Livingston Wright."

Mr. Wright was a stocky white man who worked as an anti-slavery abolitionist before his first tenure as president of the college. He spoke with a raspy cadence and often paused to clear his throat. "I'm honored to welcome you to the new academic year with added facilities. The grounds have been improved. McAdams Drive has been paved and all rooms in the older dormitories have been renovated. The new annex of Cresson Hall is an infirmary. Dr. Colston will be on the grounds continually as consulting physician."

Mr. Wright rambled on didactically for another thirty minutes. By the time he was done, it was clear that Lincoln University had high expectations for its Negro students, and Melvin, along with Nkrumah, was determined to excel.

They shared a small dormitory with a window overlooking the library on the southern end of campus. That was where they scoured through tattered pages of hand-me-down books donated by wealthier white institutions. When they weren't debating the contents of their philosophy and sociology classes, Melvin and Nkrumah played soccer, a sport Nkrumah introduced to him.

"It's called football, not soccer," Nkrumah would say exasperatedly.

"But we already have football," Melvin would protest.

"Mel, what you play in America is not football. You kick the ball once and run with it in your hands, how is that football?"

But no matter how much Nkrumah objected, Melvin insisted on calling the new sport *soccer*.

Social life on campus was nonexistent, except for a newly opened drive-in cinema on West Branch Road. Melvin invited Nkrumah one Saturday night to see the much-talked-about picture *King Kong,* starring Fay Wray and Bruce Cabot. After the end credits rolled, Nkrumah sucked his teeth and said, "This was the biggest waste of my time."

He remained apoplectic on the drive back to campus. "Why were the natives portrayed as savages? Why was the white woman King Kong's weakness?"

Needless to say, Melvin never invited Nkrumah to another picture show. On quieter nights, they traded stories about life in Virginia and the Gold Coast. Melvin talked about his hometown, Mr. Moretti's sawmill, and his decision to never go back to Virginia. Nkrumah, on the other hand, lamented about how the British controlled his country. He never failed to reiterate the historic events that led to it, and Melvin was always a captive audience.

NKRUMAH WAS BORN in the British Gold Coast, not long after the last Anglo-Ashanti war. The British had become increasingly aggressive about establishing a colony in West Africa, so they purchased the Dutch Gold Coast.

"You know why they called it the Gold Coast?" Nkrumah would ask while pacing their small dormitory.

Melvin often poked his head out from the bunk bed below: "The massive gold deposits?"

"Yes, Mel, the massive gold deposits."

Legend has it that the Portuguese discovered so much gold that they had great difficulty transporting it back home. Nkrumah's village of Nkroful was one of the jurisdictions that fell under the sale. The British colonial government soon began to expand inland, which drew the ire of the powerful Ashanti tribe. A proud empire, they refused to become a British protectorate and declared war on the crown. The British underestimated the military prowess of the Ashanti and were defeated in a bloody battle. "But you know the British, they never stop coming." Nkrumah would dramatize sipping a cup of tea with his pinky finger pointing up. Melvin, in turn, laughed hysterically. Nkrumah was right, however. The British just kept coming and soon overran the capital of the Ashanti empire, Kumasi, burning it to the ground. The Ashanti king was forced to abdicate, and he signed a promissory note to pay a sum of fifty thousand ounces of gold as indemnity to Her Majesty the Queen. Nkrumah would dig into his pocket and shake out the lint dramatically. "Now you know why I am poor, Mel."

With the Ashanti gold reserves depleted, the deposed king brokered a fragile peace treaty until an overzealous British governor did the unthinkable. Nkrumah's eyes would always go wide when he told this part of the story, whispering, as if letting Melvin in on a secret.

"Can you believe that the governor demanded the Golden Stool for him to sit on?"

"A stool made of gold?"

"Yes, solid gold. Conjured from the heavens by a powerful priest. It represented the soul of the Ashanti tribe."

"Oh shit, that ain't gonna end well," Melvin would say.

The governor's request sparked an outrage and the Queen Mother, Yaa Asantewaa, addressed the court. Nkrumah would recite her now-famous words in a rousing cadence:

> *"How can a proud and brave people like the Ashanti sit back while the white man took away their king, and humiliated them with a demand for the Golden Stool. If you, the chiefs of Ashanti, are going to behave like cowards and not fight, you should exchange your loincloths for my undergarments."*

Yaa Asantewaa then seized a gun and pulled the trigger in front of the men, and for full effect, Nkrumah would bang on the bunk bed, causing Melvin to jump.

Yaa Asantewaa led an army of five thousand soldiers, attacking the British garrisons and forts. The siege led to more than a thousand British fatalities, and it lasted for six months.

"But you know the British, they never stop coming," Nkrumah and Melvin would say in a staggered chorus.

They sent a large naval fleet, which soon overran Yaa Asantewaa's troops. She was arrested and exiled to the Seychelles, where she died. Nkrumah would conclude in a somber tone, "That is how the British became colonial masters of the Gold Coast."

No matter how many times Melvin heard the story, the ending always saddened him.

"So, how the hell you gonna kick them Brits out?"

"I don't know how, Mel, but I know I will."

ONE AFTERNOON AFTER siesta, Nkrumah came running into the dormitory with a flyer. He read the bold headline: *DO YOU HAVE WHAT IT TAKES TO BE A PHI BETA SIGMA MAN?*

"What the hell is that?" Melvin asked.

"A Greek fraternity. We should join."

"I ain't joining no damn Greeks."

"This is no ordinary fraternity," Nkrumah said, flipping through the blue Phi Beta Sigma handbook he'd found at the library. He read the text on the last page: "'Brotherhood, Scholarship, and Service.'" It took almost two weeks to convince Melvin to join him, and when he finally did, they began the intense monthlong pledging process. Between studying all facets of Greek life, hazing, and sleep deprivation, Nkrumah's health spiraled rapidly. It was not in his nature to quit, however. So Nkrumah joined his line brothers on one of their nocturnal excursions, wrapped in a blanket to ward off the piercing November cold. Their destination was a small shed on the other side of the train tracks that separated the east campus from the west.

As they approached the tracks, a loud grinding locomotive engine reverberated in the distance. The bright lights cut through the thick foliage of redwood trees and the line brothers took turns jumping over the tracks. Nkrumah was about to jump when he tripped, twisted his ankle, and landed on the steel rail. His screams were drowned out by the loud train horn and screeching metal brakes. When Melvin turned, he saw Nkrumah dragging himself across the tracks, silhouetted by the fast-approaching train. Without thinking of his own safety, Melvin grabbed Nkrumah and pulled him just before the train zoomed past. They lay paralyzed with shock, as the line brothers rushed toward them.

"I will never forget that you saved my life, Mel, I promise you that," Nkrumah quavered.

Melvin chuckled. "You better not."

The incident on the tracks strengthened Nkrumah and Melvin's bond. Two weeks later, both men pledged Phi Beta Sigma. To celebrate the milestone, a local photographer took their portraits against a large Phi Beta Sigma banner.

As MELVIN STARED at that same picture on the bus and felt the tropical Ghanaian heat, he admitted that the only person who could help them now was his old friend whose life he had saved, the president of Ghana, Kwame Nkrumah.

CHAPTER 2

Melvin felt a swaying sensation and the bus sped violently off the road. Bernadette jolted awake, amid a chorus of passengers screaming, "Jesus—Christ—Yesu—Cristo." Melvin held Bernadette tightly until the driver gained control of the bus. The lapping sounds of a burst tire soon gave way to a screeching metal rim tearing through the asphalt. As Melvin and Bernadette disembarked, each passenger shook their hands vigorously, as if a pastor's presence on the bus had somehow saved their lives. After a brief moment of shock, a heated argument broke out between the driver and a passenger, who yelled, "How you no get spare tire?"

The relatively acquiescent passengers transformed into a belligerent mob, demanding a full refund. The driver, feckless and irate, tried to dissuade the passengers to no avail. He finally paid everyone their bus fare except Melvin and Bernadette. "Pastor, I beg, if you wait here, I go run fix tire quick quick." Melvin glanced at the passengers offloading their bags.

"How far to the next station?" he asked.

The woman wearing a large headscarf scoffed. "At least two hours walking."

Bernadette shook her head defiantly.

Melvin turned to the driver. "We'll wait here, but please hurry."

He thanked them, unmounted the shredded tire, and took off running in the same direction the passengers had walked.

The scorching afternoon sun blazed through the asphalt, emitting a stomach-churning smell. The single-lane road that cut through the dense savanna had been newly constructed, and the chirps, hoots, and grunts that echoed through the tall grass were a reminder that they were far from civilization. Melvin paced back and forth, reciting a letter he intended to write President Nkrumah when they arrived in Cape Coast. He gazed nervously at the dry blades of grass and the decrepit bus that was missing one tire. "What shitty luck," he mumbled.

Bernadette sat on her suitcase with her wide-brimmed hat cocked to shield her from the sun. She began to feel nauseated and hurried to the back of the bus to throw up. Melvin, alarmed, rushed to her side. "Babe, you okay?"

"Must be something I ate. Still getting used to the food here," Bernadette replied. She rinsed her mouth with a bottle of lukewarm water and reached for a copy of *Jet* magazine she had been saving to read. The cover story was about the seldom-seen side of Eartha Kitt. There was an opinion piece about the Watts riots and a full-page advertisement for Colt 45 malt liquor and Duke hair products. A photograph of Philadelphia 76ers star Wilt Chamberlain spinning a basketball on his finger reminded Bernadette of her first date with Melvin.

IT WAS THE spring of 1964 and Bernadette had just met Melvin at the bookstore in South Philly where she worked. Melvin's boss, pleased with his performance, gave him two tickets to see the 76ers against the San Francisco Warriors. The entire city of Philadelphia was invigorated by the 76ers' recent acquisition of Wilt Chamberlain. Bernadette was, however, apathetic to sports. She had no desire to go to a basketball game, but when Melvin asked her out, she instantly accepted the invitation.

Bernadette spent most of that afternoon scouring through the closet of her quaint studio apartment for the perfect dress. She called Ella, her best friend, for styling tips, which only exacerbated her stress. After several hours and many layers of clothes spread across her sofa, she finally settled on a blue polka-dot sundress and suede tennis shoes. When Bernadette opened the door and saw Melvin holding a bouquet of lilacs, her favorite flowers, she thought right then, *I'm going to marry him*. Melvin tipped his fedora. "We can do dinner before the game if you're hungry."

They dined at Martha's Soul Food Restaurant, a popular luncheonette on Walnut Street. Melvin talked about growing up in Virginia, his time at Lincoln University, his experience in Germany fighting the Nazis, and his plans to open the first Negro-owned car dealership in Philadelphia. Bernadette, smitten by his debonair style, talked about growing up in Louisiana, her grandmother Ma' Susan, her job at the bookstore, and her dream of becoming an award-winning novelist. By the time the ice cream melted all over the peach cobbler, Melvin had asked Bernadette if it was okay to kiss her. She nodded with a shy grin, beckoning him over. Melvin slid to her side of the booth, ran his fingers gently through her hair, and kissed her forehead first. They both laughed and as the tension fell, he went for Bernadette's lips. Melvin's heart raced and his palms moistened. He had never fallen for anyone so completely, so quickly, and he wished the moment would last forever. Then the chants of swarming Warriors fans interrupted their moment of bliss. Melvin checked his watch and leapt up. "The game's about to start, Bern, we gotta go." He paid for their dinner and rushed out with Bernadette toward the Philadelphia Civic Center. Their nosebleed seats made it difficult to follow the game, but the atmosphere was electric nonetheless. Wilt Chamberlain's long-awaited debut for the 76ers was a sight to behold. He scored thirty-five points, thirty-two rebounds, and fifteen assists, sending the crowd into a frenzy. But Melvin and Bernadette wouldn't know anything about the score. They spent the better part of the game with their lips locked, only stopping to cheer when the crowd erupted.

After the game, Melvin and Bernadette spent an hour trying to hail a taxi with no luck. A slight drizzle moistened the air, and soon the rain began to pelt them.

Bernadette suggested that they take the trolley instead, which was a few blocks away.

"It'll be just like in the movies, Mel, you and me strolling under the streetlights in the rain," Bernadette said, getting a laugh out of Melvin. When the trolley finally pulled up, it was empty. Melvin helped Bernadette aboard, tipping his hat graciously. *A perfect gentleman,* Bernadette thought as she took his hand and climbed into her seat. She too had never been so easily smitten. The trolley came to a stop on Tasker Street and they stepped into the rain once more. Melvin did not let go of Bernadette's hand until they made it to her doorstep.

"Tonight was beautiful. Thank you."

Bernadette smiled. "My place is a mess, but I have a bottle of Louisiana rum we can share, if you are thirsty."

THE SOUND OF a vehicle approaching snapped Bernadette back to herself. She closed the copy of *Jet* magazine and sprang to her feet. Melvin grabbed their bags and started flagging down the vehicle. As the roaring engine got closer, Bernadette gasped. "Mel, it's a police car." Melvin froze, watching the Opel with a rotating siren pull to the side of the road. The Ghana Police emblem sent a shiver down his spine. The officer rolled down his window. "Pastor, are you okay?"

"Yes, sir—our bus got a flat tire. Driver went to fix it," Melvin quavered.

The officer smiled. "You are American?"

"Yes."

"Where to?"

"Cape Coast," Melvin said.

"Well, you are in luck. I am driving to Cape Coast now. Get in."

Melvin was too knotted up to think of an excuse, so he grabbed their bags and opened the car door for Bernadette. As she slid into her seat, Bernadette caught a whiff of stale cigarettes and diesel oil. She cracked her window slightly open to let in some air.

"I am Sergeant Asare," the officer said as he put the car in drive. He glanced at the rearview mirror and saw Melvin fixated on his Kalashnikov rifle in plain view.

"Don't worry, Pastor, I am only carrying it in case the coup plotters try to—how do you say in English—when someone don't do what you want."

"Resist?"

"Yes, resist," Sergeant Asare continued. "We have received information that the coup plotters are in Cape Coast. My officers have already located them. We will ambush tomorrow, God willing."

Melvin was distraught to hear about a coup plot against his friend President Nkrumah. He had only read about his great accomplishments in the newspapers since they arrived in Ghana. What Melvin didn't know was that in the few years after Nkrumah won Ghana's independence, several attempts on his life had made him paranoid. His main development project, the Akosombo hydroelectric dam, had forced him to align with Russia. This angered both America and Great Britain. They supported the opposition's plans to overthrow him. He, in turn, consolidated power, banned all political parties, and declared himself president for life.

"You are lucky that I stopped," Sergeant Asare said. "There are many thieves on this road. That is why the driver left you to watch his bus. By the time he returns, the rest of the tires will be gone."

Melvin wasn't paying attention. The news about Nkrumah had triggered another throbbing headache. He searched his memories for any despotic signs he might have missed. Bernadette eyed him worriedly as she crossed and uncrossed her legs until he placed a hand on one, stilling them both.

A crackle from the police walkie-talkie interrupted Melvin's pondering.

"You have a church in America?" Sergeant Asare asked.

"Yes, in Philadelphia," Bernadette replied.

"Ah—Philadelphia."

"You have been there?"

"No—I met a doctor from Philadelphia during the war."

"Really?" Melvin asked, feigning curiosity.

SERGEANT ASARE HAD served in the British Commonwealth army during the Second World War. He joined a hundred thousand African soldiers conscripted to fight the Nazis and the imperial Japanese army.

"Can you imagine the colonized fighting on behalf of the colonizer to protect the colonizer from being colonized?" Sergeant Asare said in a succinct rehearsed tone, clearly a phrase he had repeated more than once.

"You see, the white men were afraid of the jungle in Asia, so we the African regiment had to carry their ammo, create roads for their tanks, and fight on the front line."

Sergeant Asare glanced at his captive audience in the rearview mirror.

"That is where I get this," he said, lifting up his service cap to reveal a thick scar across his scalp. "If it wasn't for that doctor from Philadelphia, I would have died."

Melvin stared at the scar and was tempted to trade stories about his own experience in Germany during the war, but he thought it wise to stay quiet.

"And can you believe that when we returned, the British refused to pay us?"

"Really?" Bernadette asked, now enthralled by the story.

"Yes, they said the colonial government had no money and they closed the war office."

"So what happened?"

"We marched, and they shot our leaders. Then they declare—how do you say in English, when the military makes a certain time for you to be in your house?"

"Curfew?"

"Yes, they declare curfew. That is when Osagyefo arrived."

OSAGYEFO, WHICH LOOSELY translated into "Redeemer," was Kwame Nkrumah's title given to him by his followers. He had just returned to the Gold Coast after many years studying in America. His arrival coincided with the massive protests and civil disobedience instigated by the veterans. Being the master orator that he was, Nkrumah galvanized the disgruntled soldiers and turned their grievances into an independence movement.

"So they arrest him, and we elect him prime minister while still in prison. After that the British had no choice. They granted us full independence. And now they are working with the coup plotters to overthrow him? I will not allow it."

The bright headlights of the police car caught a shadowy figure running on the side of the road. Bernadette glanced to see the bus driver, still racing with the shredded tire. Sergeant Asare shook his head apologetically. "Look at this foolish driver, giving all Ghanaians a bad name."

IT WAS EARLY evening when the police car pulled into town. A streetlight brightened a wretched sign that read *WELCOME TO CAPE COAST.*

The roads were deserted except for a few growling stray dogs who reminded the townspeople that they ruled the night. Ahead in the distance, a kaleidoscope of lights emanated from fishing canoes, only outdone by the flashing police car headlights. Sergeant Asare checked the rearview mirror and caught Melvin and Bernadette's reflection. "I am very hungry," he said in an exhausted tone. "You must be hungry too." Melvin glanced at Bernadette anxiously. She thought about declining the offer for food, but her stomach rumblings were almost audible over the car engine, so she replied, "Yes, some food would be nice."

THE CHOP BAR was buzzing with hordes of nocturnal patrons. Most were boys who acted old enough to be men, and men who acted young enough to be boys. The riffraff of Cape Coast who congregated with a single agenda: Whose television set would be next to disappear? Needless to say, the sight of a uniformed police officer and two Americans in the chop bar gave everyone pause. A sudden silence descended on the dimly lit den as the patrons stretched their necks. The flickering fluorescent tube that hung from the corrugated roof did little to brighten the menu, which was scribbled on the wall in chalk. Sergeant Asare, tired of squinting to read the menu, finally called for the proprietress. She had been hiding behind the counter because she was operating without a license. Satisfied that she wasn't the target of an arrest, she strolled out and beamed. "Akwaaba, Officer. My best waitress, Araba, will prepare a table for you and your guests." Taking a cue from the proprietress's cozy interaction with Sergeant Asare, the riffraff resumed their scheming chatter. Araba, the young waitress, squeezed between two tables balancing a tray of empty bottles in one hand and a steaming pot of fufu in the other.

"Your table is ready, sah," Araba said, as she ushered Sergeant Asare to a squalid set of furniture. She turned to Bernadette. "Beer, Coke, or water for you, madam?"

"Water," Bernadette replied, awestruck by Araba's appearance. She bore an uncanny resemblance to Ella, Bernadette's best friend of fifteen years. Araba cleared her throat. "We only have the chicken special—is chicken okay?"

"Yes," Bernadette replied.

"And for you, sah?"

"Same," Melvin echoed.

As Araba turned to leave, Bernadette stood abruptly. "Is there a restroom I can use?"

"A room to rest?"

"No—she wants a toilet," Sergeant Asare snarled.

"Oh, sorry. Toilet is behind the building," Araba said, pointing to the back door.

ALL EYES WERE on Bernadette as she meandered toward the narrow passage clogged with boxes, utensils, and other random objects that had no business in a restaurant hallway. As she approached the back door, a dizzy spell stunned her, and she clutched the walls. Bernadette felt a sharp pain in her stomach and stumbled outside, waiting until it subsided. The cubicle stood adjacent to the restaurant and was lit by a lantern that was missing a handle. As Bernadette approached the roofless structure, a young woman brushed past her. "Careful, sister. It is slippery in there."

The lantern cast a large shadow on Bernadette as she searched for the edge of the toilet. The stench of stale piss reminded Bernadette of Baton Rouge, and her best friend Ella.

ELLA MAXINE TURNER was sixteen when she transferred to La Salle High School. Her father, a devout Catholic, had been selected to be the first Negro librarian at the seminary in Baton Rouge, and so he uprooted his whole family from Houston, Texas. Ella's first week at La Salle was hell. She had no friends and ate alone at a solitary table in the cafeteria. Bernadette noticed Ella during their lunch breaks and empathized with her. So, one day, she decided to join Ella at the lunch counter.

"I wouldn't touch that meatloaf if I was you," Bernadette whispered. "Heaven knows what's in that thing."

No one had spoken to Ella since she set foot on La Salle's campus, so she was completely thrown off by Bernadette.

"You talking to me?"

"I don't see no one else tryna get that meatloaf 'cept you."

Ella exhaled. "You're right. That meatloaf do look suspicious."

"I'm Bernadette, you can call me Bern." Bernadette balanced her tray under her arm and shook Ella's hand.

"I'm Ella. Nice to meet you."

The two girls sat at the table and ate, talked, and laughed until the obnoxiously loud bell cleared the cafeteria of all the chattering students.

"I guess I'll see you after class," Bernadette said as the girls split down the hallway.

Bernadette and Ella became inseparable after that. They walked home together every day after school and talked about all the things teenage girls in Baton Rouge obsessed about: boys.

They gossiped about who was cute, and who would ask them out to prom. On occasion, they talked about their dreams. Ella envisioned herself on stage singing in a jazz quintet. Bernadette, who had become obsessed with her English literature class, dreamt of being a novelist. She talked endlessly about her favorite writers, Zora Neale Hurston and Gwendolyn Brooks.

"You got ambition, Bern, you gonna be somebody," Ella would say.

On weekends, Ella invited Bernadette over for dinner, after which she routinely apologized for her parents' obsessive Catholic traditions, like reciting the rosary before every meal. Quite the contrary, Bernadette was in awe of Ella's family. A household with a father and mother was a revelation to her, and although she appreciated her grandmother Ma' Susan, she wished she had what Ella had.

As the school year wore on, and the roller coaster that was twelfth grade seemed to taper off, the question of what college the girls should apply to became imminent. Ella's father took it upon himself to suggest Villa Maria Catholic College in Philadelphia, a women's college founded by the Sisters of the Immaculate Heart of Mary.

"Good Catholic girls go to good Catholic schools," he said at the dinner table.

"But Paw, Bern ain't even Catholic," Ella shot back.

"Don't worry about it, sweetheart, I'll talk to Ma' Susan myself."

But Ma' Susan's health had deteriorated rapidly and in spite of many doctor visits, there was still no definite diagnosis of her condition. The once vibrant shotgun house that was redolent with the aroma of Ma' Susan's famous shrimp gumbo and the sonic wizardry of Count Basie's orchestra had now been reduced to a grim, desolate convalescent home. Ma' Susan's condition took an enormous toll on Bernadette. Her grades suffered and her savings dried up. It was now Ella's turn to spend time at Bernadette's house. She helped with chores and cared for Ma' Susan while Bernadette went job hunting. Their emotional whirlwind crescendoed after graduation, when both girls received acceptance letters and scholarships to Villa Maria College. Bernadette, unable to leave Ma' Susan's side, decided to take a year off to find work. Much to the anger and frustration of her parents, Ella decided to do the same in solidarity with her best friend. That was how Bernadette and Ella's adventure at El Ray's began.

EL RAY'S WAS a popular jazz club in the heart of Baton Rouge owned by Ray Riboud, a fast-talking swindler. The club stood on the corner of Gus Young Avenue and Columbus Dunn Drive. It attracted the best jazz musicians and a steady clientele. This was until a local businessman opened a jazz club across the street. Within a month, most of Ray's patrons had switched over to the more sophisticated Club Le Rouge. Ray's financial woes compounded when the banks threatened to foreclose on his property.

That was the pending doom swirling through Ray's mind on that Saturday morning when Bernadette and Ella strolled in. "What can I do you for?" Ray asked without raising his gaze from the newspaper he pretended to read.

Bernadette cleared her throat. "Morning, sir. We was wondering if you was looking for some waitresses." Ray looked up, his eyes cutting across the girls as if inspecting a piece of merchandise.

"You see anyone here that need waiting on?"

"No, sir," Bernadette replied, now regretting that they had come all this way. Just as they turned to leave, Ray asked, "Can ya sang?"

"No," Bernadette replied. "But my friend can."

Bernadette nudged Ella, who nodded abashedly.

"Well, since my singer done run off to that whorehouse

across the street masquerading as a jazz club, you ladies might be in luck."

Ray called his pianist and auditioned Ella that morning. Even Bernadette was blown away by her voice. Ray, ecstatic that he had discovered the next big thing, hired Ella on the spot and gave Bernadette a job behind the bar. Within a few weeks El Ray's experienced a rebirth. Ella and her band were a hit among the younger college crowd. Bernadette earned a staggering amount of tips, so much that she hired extra help to care for Ma' Susan. Things were going well until the owner of Club Le Rouge decided to woo Ella to his club. He courted her, doubled her pay, and made Ella the Tuesday night head-liner, a coveted slot for all the bands in town. Bernadette tried to convince Ella to stay at El Ray's, but she wouldn't budge. She needed the money after her parents kicked her out of the house for singing the "devil's music." This was the last straw for Ray.

It was one thing to open a competing business across the street, but to steal his main act? That was a declaration of war. So one night, after an extended episode of drinking, Ray broke into Club Le Rouge, unzipped his pants, pulled out his pecker, and sprayed every visible surface. The carpets, the ta-bles, the stage, nothing was spared. And to crown it all, he climbed atop the Steinway piano and took a glorious dump on the ivory keys.

This forced Club Le Rouge to close down, and Ella de-cided it was time to enroll at Villa Maria Catholic College. On the day she left for Philadelphia, Bernadette accompanied her to the bus depot and as they walked down Gus Young Ave-nue, the stench of stale shit and piss was still terrorizing pe-destrians.

. . .

A KNOCK ON the janky cubicle door brought Bernadette back to the present.

"I beg—I have to go," a desperate voice yelled from behind the door.

"One minute, please," Bernadette shouted as she pulled down her dress. She opened the door and a woman rushed past her into the cubicle. Bernadette washed her hands and walked back into the restaurant. Melvin, an utter bundle of nerves, leapt up and pulled Bernadette's chair out for her.

"You okay, babe? You was gone for a while," he whispered.

"I'm fine, Mel," Bernadette replied as she stared at the grilled chicken for which she had lost her appetite.

AFTER THEIR MEAL, Sergeant Asare drove Melvin and Bernadette to Paradise Hotel, a secluded beachfront lodge near the famed Elmina Castle. The lobby boy, caught in a splash of headlights, ran to welcome the guests. Bernadette thanked Sergeant Asare and followed the lobby boy into the foyer. Melvin grabbed their luggage. "Thank you for the ride, be careful tomorrow."

Sergeant Asare smiled. "In my village we say, only a fool checks the depth of a river with both feet. My officers have taken all precautions, Pastor. By tomorrow the coup plotters will be in jail. I can promise you that."

Sergeant Asare put the car in drive and sped off, leaving Melvin in a fog of exhaust fumes. News of a coup plot against Nkrumah was deeply unsettling. The main reason he'd fled to Ghana with Bernadette was because he believed Nkrumah could protect them. Now, he wasn't so sure.

The lobby boy interrupted Melvin's brooding. "Hello, sah? Your wife needs you inside." Melvin followed the boy into the foyer, where Bernadette stood frazzled.

"They need our passports to check us in, honey."

Melvin's face collapsed. He remembered that in their hasty escape from Accra, they had forgotten to claim their passports from the front desk receptionist. He pretended to dig in his bags for the passports, and Bernadette pretended to be angry at him. "He always does this," she said, rolling her eyes. The bald man behind the desk tapped his pen impatiently. "Pastor, do you have the passport, or not?"

"It's here somewhere," Melvin said, still digging.

Then he leaned closer to the bald man and whispered, "My wife is very tired. Can you check us in, and I'll bring the passports down in the morning?"

The man appeared resistant, and then he acquiesced. "I only do this because you are pastor. But I need passport in morning, sah." Melvin thanked him with a generous tip, and they hurried to their room, collapsing on the spring mattress.

CHAPTER 3

The musty Cape Coast humidity woke Melvin. He squinted, eyes adjusting to the harsh sunlight bursting through the window. Then he wiped the sweat from his brow and glanced to see Bernadette sitting in a bamboo chair half naked. Her eyes were fixed on the crashing waves in the distance. Melvin rolled out of bed, lit a cigarette, and took a light drag. He let out the smoke in thick, shapeless puffs. A sense of calm descended on him. One he hadn't felt since they fled Philadelphia. Then he remembered why they were running in the first place. Images flashed through his mind. The rain, the broken glass, the weight of the gun, the blood that splattered the concrete. Melvin's hands began to tremble. No, he wouldn't get sucked into another wave of depression.

He walked over to Bernadette and kissed her neck gently. She let out a deep sigh as Melvin wrapped his hands around her, soothing and reassuring. A soft guitar melody seeped through their window. Melvin drew the curtains curiously. He leaned out to see a group of men hanging a large banner outside the hotel courtyard. When the banner was finally hoisted, it read *KWESI KWAYSON & HIS DYNAMO BAND*.

"Sleep well, Bern?" Melvin asked as he extinguished the cigarette against the windowsill.

Bernadette shook her head. "Not really."

"I know it's rough, babe, but it'll all work out, I promise. All we gotta do is get to the president and everything will be fine."

Melvin's assured tone had a calming effect on Bernadette. He gently took her by the hand and led her to the bed, where they remained wrapped around each other until the music blaring from the courtyard piqued their interest.

"What if someone recognizes us?" Bernadette asked as she threw a scarf over her head.

"Nah, babe, we far from the city now. Plus we ain't the only foreigners here," Melvin replied, adjusting his Ray-Ban glasses to conceal his face.

They discreetly joined the other hotel patrons in awe of Ghana's number-one highlife band performing in the court-yard. The masterful horn choreography, fiery drum shuffles, and electric guitar hypnotized the crowd. At first, Bernadette resisted. But after three songs, she dragged Melvin to the dance floor and they too were swept up in the hysteria. It was a moment of release they both needed, the tension in their bones somewhat dissipating. Bernadette had never heard music like this before. The polyphonic African rhythms blar-ing out of the speakers were nothing like the jazz and blues she was used to in America. But somehow it all felt familiar. The melodies were intoxicating and she felt a natural high. Bernadette spun, twisted, and shuffled to every guitar lick that reverberated from the stage. The warmth of the sound seemed to encapsulate and give meaning to all that she couldn't say in words, and when she looked up, she caught the eyes of the lead guitarist and singer, Kwesi Kwayson.

Kwesi froze, attempted to strum his guitar, but his hands wouldn't move. He wasn't a stranger to seeing beautiful women fall under the spell of his guitar, but this was different. It seemed that he was under his own spell now. Kwesi stared at Bernadette, the sway in her hips, the graceful strut; she commanded attention. She, in turn, did not look away. An otherworldly glow thrust Kwesi and Bernadette into an orbit of their own, morphing time into a nebulous fog. Bernadette found herself floating into Kwesi's arms while the entire crowd remained still. Then she jolted awake from her trance to see Melvin tugging on her arm. "You okay, babe?"

"I feel light-headed," Bernadette muttered.

Melvin helped her back to their table. He lit a cigarette and kept his eyes on Bernadette, who kept her eyes on Kwesi. The band performed their hit song "Mami Wata Highlife," and Kwesi belted out the lyrics:

"Mami Wata, Mami Wata,
My love for you no be small mata,
This guitar you carry give me oh,
I go sing until we marry oh,
Mami Wata, Mami Wata,
Mami Wata, Mami Wata."

A horde of wealthy patrons flooded the dance floor dressed in colorful batik prints. It was obvious that most of the rich men had snuck out with their mistresses, and yet they couldn't resist the urge to show off. They plastered ten-cedi notes across Kwesi's forehead as he contorted to the final refrain of the song. There was an enormous amount of money on stage when Kwesi finished. His band had to carry him off to avoid stepping on the banknotes. The crowd burst into loud applause, hoping for an encore, which never happened.

Melvin turned to see a group of white men dressed in black suits congregated around the bar. He panicked, then turned swiftly to avoid making eye contact. Had the FBI tracked them down to Cape Coast? Had they come to arrest him and Bernadette? Just then, one of the men ordered his drink in a thick Russian accent and Melvin sighed, deeply relieved.

Bernadette, still disoriented, excused herself.

"I'll be up soon," Melvin said, watching Bernadette disappear into the crowd. He took another gulp from his glass of whiskey, a brand that tasted similar to the moonshine his father left sitting around the house. The polychromatic lights on stage caught Melvin's eyes and his life seemed to flash before him. In that moment, he surmised that his entire existence till this point had been a constant flight from his father's shadow. His decision to go to college, to enlist in the war, and every other major decision in his life were somehow linked to his father, Earl. In his moment of clarity, Melvin envisioned himself as a father. What would life be once they were finally safe and no longer seeking refuge? Could they return to life as normal? Build a family here? He quickly banished the thought from his mind. Of course, he knew Bernadette would be a great mother. She often spoke about having a family, creating what she never had. But Melvin didn't trust himself to be any better than his father; he feared he'd make the same mistakes.

. . .

WHEN BERNADETTE REACHED the room, she pulled out the ornate leather-bound diary she had neglected to use since they arrived in Ghana. It was one of the few items she cherished and would not burn as they decided what to keep and what to part with. Bernadette neatly scribbled in cursive:

January 2nd, 1966
Something weird happened to me today, and I can't explain it. I just met a man and it felt like an out-of-body experience. As if I had known him my whole life. Ghana is full of these strange encounters, but this one feels different. . . .

THE EARLY-MORNING SUN had flooded the sky when Bernadette made her way downstairs for breakfast. Melvin was still nursing a dreadful hangover. When Bernadette asked if he would join her, he mumbled something undecipherable in a groggy tone. Bernadette descended the stairs cautiously, avoiding the bald man behind the reception desk who was still waiting for their passports. She sat in the beautifully manicured courtyard overlooking the Elmina Castle.

A young server laid a white cloth on Bernadette's table. "Tea and today's newspaper for you, madam?"

Bernadette nodded and was served a cup of vaporous Lipton tea. The bold newspaper headline caught her attention: *POLICE OFFICER KILLED BY COUP PLOTTERS.* Bernadette gasped when she recognized Sergeant Asare's photo. *Dammit,* she thought. He was such a kind man. They could still be stranded on that road if he hadn't offered them a ride to Cape Coast. After gathering her composure, Bernadette read the details of how Sergeant Asare was killed:

THE DAILY GRAPHIC

January 3rd, 1966

At approximately 8 pm last night, Police Sergeant Kofi Asare from the Greater Accra Precinct was killed by alleged coup plotters in Cape Coast. Sergeant Asare and his officers had ambushed a suspected hideout near Mankessim. The coup plotters were preparing to overthrow President Nkrumah's government. Assistant Police Chief Komla Amegavie announced today that there will be a state burial for Sergeant Asare. He is survived by his wife, Ama Asare, and their three children.

Bernadette thought about running upstairs to tell Melvin about Sergeant Asare's death, but when she looked up, she saw Kwesi walking toward her. "Do you mind if I join you?" he asked with a smile that stilled her.

Bernadette wanted to say no, but the only word that rolled out of her mouth was a small, feeble "Sure." Kwesi slid into the chair across from Bernadette. He was more handsome than she remembered from the night before. Maybe it was the sunlight reflecting off his dark skin or his thick eyebrows that furrowed when he smiled wistfully at her. His athletic build and chiseled jawline enthralled Bernadette, and she did her best to avert her eyes.

"Have we met?" Kwesi asked.

"No," she said, almost too quickly. Then regretted it. "I mean—I don't know where we could have met."

Kwesi nodded as he lit a cigarette. "Of course, you are not from here."

"No," she answered.

"America?"

Bernadette nodded.

"I could tell from the way you were dancing last night."

"Oh, really? You probably say the same thing to every girl you meet." Bernadette chuckled.

Kwesi smiled and doused the cigarette in a wooden ashtray emblazoned with burn marks. "My name is Kwesi," he said, shaking Bernadette's hand. He let his fingers slowly linger as he retrieved his hand from hers.

There was a kinetic spark between the two of them, and Bernadette couldn't remember any of the fake names she had rehearsed for a moment like this, so she just muttered, "Bernadette, my name is Bernadette."

"Was that your husband dancing with you last night?"

Bernadette hesitated. "Yes, but we're more like, you know, engaged."

"Ah, I see. What brings you here?"

"We're opening a church, my fiancé is a pastor," Bernadette said, keeping up with the lie.

"Really? I would have never guessed that you were engaged to a pastor," Kwesi opined, studying her. Bernadette was eager to change the subject. Just then, a waiter interrupted them with a steamy cup of tea. When the vapor cleared, Bernadette said, "Your band was amazing last night. I've never heard music like that before."

"It's called highlife," Kwesi replied, describing the harmonies that distinguished the sound from popular Western music. As Bernadette listened to Kwesi, she gazed at his lips, and she wondered how good they must be to kiss. She let herself disappear into the fantasy, even if only for a brief moment. Incidentally, Kwesi was thinking the same thing about Bernadette as she took a sip of her tea. There was an uncomfortable pause, and they both averted their eyes at the same time, slightly embarrassed, as if they could read each other's minds. Bernadette quickly filled the awkward silence.

"How long have you been playing?"

"Me? Since I was a child."

Kwesi took a gulp of his scalding hot tea. His mind catapulted to his earliest memories as he recounted his story to Bernadette.

Kwesi Kwayson was born in a small village near Cape Coast. His father, a cocoa farmer, disavowed responsibility and swore by the gods of thunder and lightning to strike him down if he was Kwesi's father. The next day, while harvesting his cocoa pods, lightning struck through his farm. His charred body was found a week later crawling with maggots.

Kwesi's mother was the proprietress of a popular palm wine bar near the market. Her palm wine was rumored to be the best in town and her legend grew among the local farmers, fishermen, and retired soldiers.

One such soldier was Agya Ko, a World War II veteran and virtuoso guitarist. He had a brief successful music career, but after a string of bad luck, he wasted away in the labyrinth of insobriety. When he had too much to drink, Agya Ko picked up his guitar and lamented about his problems. The discordant melodies enchanted Kwesi. He skipped many chores at the bar to listen to Agya Ko, much to his mother's dismay. Kwesi got in the habit of trading free palm wine for guitar lessons every time his mother went to the market for firewood. She started to notice the subtle pilfering and decided to set a trap.

One day, she tied her scarf, said goodbye to Kwesi, and hid across the street. Just as she suspected, Agya Ko came strolling in with his guitar hoisted across his shoulder. Kwesi served him free palm wine, and in turn, Agya Ko taught him the harmonic minor scales. Kwesi's mother waited for Agya Ko to exit the bar before she pounced on him and gave him a good thrashing. She saved the worst beating for Kwesi. The lacerations on his calves the next morning were proof. But that didn't stop Kwesi's obsession with the guitar.

As soon as he was old enough, Kwesi got a job at the Cape Coast port hauling sacks of cocoa onto freight ships. He found the working conditions abhorrent, and the pittance he was paid made a mockery of the backbreaking work he and the other head porters endured. But the pay was enough to buy a used guitar, which was missing two strings and had no tuning pegs.

When Kwesi wasn't practicing or loading cocoa he spent his time on the ship deck doing menial jobs for the sailors, most of whom were American. That was where he learned to speak English. He befriended a soft-spoken Negro sailor named Eddy Jones.

As a parting gift before heading back to America, Eddy bequeathed him a portable phonograph player. The only record Eddy gave Kwesi was the 1951 Louis Armstrong album *Satchmo at Pasadena*. Kwesi played that album until the grooves wore out, causing it to skip every time "The Hucklebuck" played. He learned every guitar riff and could impersonate Louis's deep baritone voice flawlessly. Kwesi pictured himself dressed in a white tuxedo and black bow tie performing at the Copacabana. He imagined crowds of elegant women cheering as Louis Armstrong introduced his star guitarist from the Gold Coast.

Kwesi's dream was America, and nothing was going to stop him. So, on that warm rainy night, when the transistor radio broadcast that Louis Armstrong was set to visit the Gold Coast, Kwesi took it as a good omen. Brimming with excitement, he packed his guitar and a few belongings, said goodbye to his mother, and waited at the bus depot. When the boneshaker bus finally arrived, it was packed with goats, cows, and local herders heading to Accra for the market day. Kwesi held his breath for most of the journey to curtail the stench emanating from the livestock. After five torturous hours, the boneshaker passed a sign that read WELCOME TO BRITISH JAMESTOWN ACCRA.

Kwesi stuck his head out the window, marveling at the tall buildings and automobiles that populated the capital city. A few British Union Jack flags billowed atop flagpoles as the boneshaker eased to a stop. Kwesi joined the hordes of people waiting to welcome Satchmo. The sounds of a DC-8 aircraft sent the crowd into a frenzy and the man of the hour, Louis Armstrong, stepped off the plane. He carried a trumpet in one hand and a white handkerchief in the other. When he waved, a rapturous feeling overcame Kwesi. He gazed at his hero's motorcade, zooming down the dusty Accra road.

That night, Louis Armstrong mesmerized thousands of fans with straight-ahead jazz and big band compositions. After the concert, Kwesi, elated, remembered that he had made no sleeping arrangements. He strolled to the Accra port and joined the head porters who had set up a small encampment in anticipation of a freight ship scheduled to dock at sunrise.

Kwesi tossed and turned on the folded cardboard that night, unable to sleep. He was tormented by the shadows of dreams unfulfilled. As he gazed at the constellations scattered across the sky, Kwesi decided right then that he would stow away on the next ship heading to America.

Early the next morning, Kwesi joined the queue of head porters in awe of the colossal vessel. They took turns flipping cocoa sacks onto canoes and battling the waves until they offloaded the cargo on the ship deck. The ship captain was a burly Texan who spat tobacco residue into a metal cup when he spoke.

"Any y'all speak English?" he yelled from across the deck.

Kwesi raised his hand timidly.

"Awlright, you get paid extra to count these here bags."

KWESI SPENT THE entire afternoon tallying the cocoa sacks and scouting the cargo unit for a discreet hiding place. When the night sky descended on the port, he snuck his guitar, a jerry can of water, and a bag of roasted groundnuts aboard the ship. Kwesi tucked himself behind a mountain of cocoa sacks and crouched into a fetal position. Was this really happening? Was his dream finally coming true? Kwesi remembered that he had asked Eddy Jones how long the voyage to America took. Eddy had paused shaving, wiped the blade slowly on a towel, and replied, "Three weeks, hell, sometimes four. It just depend on how calm the seas is."

When the ship's horn blared and the light swaying began, Kwesi prayed to the gods of his ancestors for calm seas. And that was what he got for the first seven days hiding in the belly of the gargantuan vessel. Apart from the slight seasickness that left him nauseated on the first night, the journey had been relatively uneventful.

To pass time, Kwesi practiced a series of arpeggios on his guitar, playing in a muted tone, barely audible to himself. But in the second week, the ship hit a tempestuous storm, and the violent crashing waves toppled the cocoa sacks above Kwesi. He was lucky to escape unscathed, but his jerry can tipped over, burst open, and flooded the rusty cargo floor. After a few days, the dehydration became unbearable. So when Kwesi heard the rattling rain droplets one night, he wagered the risk was worth it. He snuck onto the slippery deck and just when he thought the coast was clear, a large hand grabbed his shoulder. Kwesi turned swiftly and a thrusting punch shattered his jaw, causing him to black out. When he gained consciousness, he was lying in a sludgy mix of blood and rainwater. His eyes fluttered, catching the silhouette of the ship captain, who spat in his metal cup.

"You tryna catch a free ride to America, boy?" he muttered, while chewing his tobacco.

Kwesi squinted, unable to see the shadowy men crowded behind their captain. One of the men yelled, "Ain't nobody else in there. Just this here lousy gitar."

The captain grinned maliciously. His gold tooth glistened. "Well, I guess it was nice meeting you." The captain turned to his men. "Get this nigger off my ship."

Kwesi thought about fighting back, but he knew his fate was sealed. The men grabbed him by the limbs, hoisted him above the ship's stern, and flung him overboard. Kwesi splashed into the crashing waves. His body slowly descended into an abyss of endless darkness.

"You're so full of shit," Bernadette chuckled. "That's not a true story."

"I swear it happened just like I'm telling you," Kwesi said.

"So, how are you still alive?" Bernadette asked, trying to suppress a laugh.

"Mami Wata," Kwesi replied, taking a sip of his now lukewarm tea.

"Mami Wata?"

"Yes, Mami Wata. You probably call her a mermaid. That is who saved my life."

Bernadette burst out laughing. "I'm sorry, it's just that my grandmother was obsessed with mermaids and I never thought I'd meet someone who believed in them too."

Kwesi waited for Bernadette's laughter to taper off, and then he told her the rest of his story:

After the sailors threw him overboard, Kwesi's body grew limp and sank to the bottom of the ocean. A shimmering glow engulfed his vision and he assumed that he had crossed into the afterlife. Then a silhouette of a mermaid appeared in the glimmer. Her thick gray locs floated behind her as she swam closer to Kwesi. She touched his forehead and the coral reefs illuminated. The mermaid reached into the reef and conjured the most beautiful guitar Kwesi had ever seen. It was made of silver and the string pegs were made of gold. "This is yours," the mermaid thundered. Kwesi's eyes gleamed as the guitar floated toward him. He reached out to touch it and the mermaid's voice echoed once more. "This is your destiny. You must play this guitar on the eve of Ghana's independence. Not a day before and not a day after."

Kwesi repeated her words. "Not a day before and not a day after."

He grabbed the guitar and the sea collapsed into a dark void, causing him to lose consciousness. When Kwesi woke up, he was surrounded by a group of fishermen staring curiously at him. They thought he was dead and had begun casting their lots to see who would get the glistening guitar that washed ashore with him. Their collective gasp gave way to disappointment when Kwesi stood up, picked up the guitar, and staggered down the Cape Coast shore. He stayed indoors for a week, trying to make sense of what had happened. He remembered the mammoth ship, the tobacco-chewing captain, the unruly sailors who threw him overboard, the mermaid with gray locs, the silver guitar, and the words that loomed menacingly over him: "Not a day before and not a day after." But Kwesi couldn't resist the allure of the guitar. He had heard of many highlife bands that scored hits after supernatural encounters like the one he had just experienced. It was rumored that mystical dwarfs, humanoid birds, and mermaids bestowed fame and wealth on musicians, and Kwesi was desperate for both. Yes, he could wait for independence eve to play the guitar, but no one could predict when the British would finally loosen their colonial grip on the Gold Coast.

Kwesi paced anxiously in his room until he finally gave in. He plugged the guitar into his amplifier and struck a chord, timidly. Then he waited, but nothing happened. He closed his eyes, slid his fingers across the frets, and played an arpeggio. When Kwesi opened his eyes, the room was swirling with a cascade of flowers, floating in a pulsating spiral.

. . .

"FLOWERS?" BERNADETTE ASKED, baffled.

"Yes, flowers. That was the day I wrote 'Mami Wata Highlife,' and it became a hit."

"So you didn't listen to the supposed mermaid?"

"I played the guitar on the eve of independence just as she asked."

"But the magical lady with a tail said not a day before, and not a day after." Bernadette was making light, teasing even, but she didn't really think much of it.

"For someone who doesn't believe my story, you're asking a lot of questions." Kwesi shrugged with a sly smile.

"MAMI WATA HIGHLIFE" catapulted Kwesi to instant stardom. He was invited to perform at the Ghana Broadcasting Corporation, which garnered the largest audience in the country. Newly elected President Nkrumah heard "Mami Wata Highlife" and invited Kwesi to perform at his gala for Queen Elizabeth.

Bernadette's eyes lit up when she heard Nkrumah's name. "You performed for the president?"

"Yes. In fact, we are on our way to perform for him next week in Kulungugu."

"Where's that?"

"It is in the Northern Region. We leave tomorrow for a three-day drive."

Bernadette was about to inquire about the journey when she saw Melvin walking toward them. "Nice to see you two getting acquainted."

"I was just leaving," Kwesi stammered, smothering his cigarette.

"No. Please, stay, I insist."

Bernadette tried to ease the tension. "Kwesi is performing for the president next week, Mel."

Melvin instantly sobered up. "You're performing for Nkrumah? Where at?"

"Kulungugu. It's a three-day drive from here."

This was the best news Melvin had heard in days. None of the letters he had written President Nkrumah had garnered a response, so he asked forthrightly, "Can we join you on the trip?"

"To Kulungugu?"

"Yes, we can pay our way if—" Melvin started to say, and then Kwesi cut him off.

"It's not the money. I just didn't plan on traveling with anyone. Besides, you are here to open a new church, no?"

Melvin leaned forward, putting on his most convincing face. "We just want to see the real Ghana before we begin our missionary work. This road trip sounds like a great experience."

Kwesi hesitated, pondering his dilemma. He was undoubtedly smitten by Bernadette, and relished the idea of traveling with her. But Kwesi's upcoming performance for President Nkrumah wasn't just another show. It was an audition of sorts, for the opportunity to join the president's official band on a cultural exchange to North America, a dream Kwesi still held on to. He worried that letting Bernadette and Melvin tag along could derail his plans, but Kwesi was so enchanted by Bernadette that he acquiesced. "All right, I will show you the real Ghana, if that's what you want. But I suggest we start here." He pointed at the large stone walls of Elmina Castle. "Can you be ready in two hours?"

Bernadette grinned. "Of course."

Kwesi nodded and strolled off.

When he was out of earshot, Melvin turned to Bernadette and whispered, in an unambiguous tone, "I think he has a thing for you."

Bernadette rolled her eyes. "Don't start with that, Mel, please."

Melvin knew exactly what she meant. Any man who did as little as glance at Bernadette was accused of trying to steal her from him. So when they returned to their room, Melvin began to have second thoughts. He knew that meeting President Nkrumah would end their nightmare, but did it have to be through Kwesi? Was there another way? Bernadette could sense his apprehension. "We ain't come this far to get cold feet, Mel," she said as she slid into her silk fitted dress that Melvin had tried to dissuade her from wearing.

"Nah, just wondering if we can trust him is all."

"What other choice we have? He's going to meet the president. We going to meet the president too. Sound like God's blessing if you ask me." Melvin wasn't paying attention. He was staring disapprovingly at Bernadette's dress, which accentuated her full hips.

"Do it gotta be that tight, babe?" Melvin finally asked. But Bernadette had picked the dress for that exact reason. She wanted Kwesi to see what she looked like dressed up, a harmless wanting. She had no intention of going further than that. It had been a while since anyone looked at her the way Kwesi did, and she just wanted to blur her troubles some. So she smiled at Melvin and said, "I love you, Mel, but I ain't dressing how you want."

CHAPTER 4

Melvin and Bernadette descended cautiously into the lobby and were relieved to see a young lady behind the reception desk instead of the bald man. She smiled politely and didn't ask them for their passports. Kwesi was sitting in the front seat of a taxi adjusting the lens of his Pentax camera when Melvin and Bernadette stepped out.

"Stop right there," he shouted. "Okay, I'm ready. Smile."

The camera shutter clicked in rapid succession. Bernadette grinned, leaning closer to Melvin, who just stared lethargically. Kwesi had the urge to compliment Bernadette's silk fitted dress, but he knew better. So instead he said, "The castle closes in two hours. We have to go now."

Melvin was pensive for most of the drive, occasionally hurling a snarky comment when the conversation between Kwesi and Bernadette broke out in rapturous laughter. He had told himself that Kwesi was merely a means to an end. All he had to do was survive the three-day journey to Nkrumah, but that didn't help him conceal his angst. Kwesi, on the other hand, was impervious to the tension. He basked in Bernadette's light and she relished the attention, if only a small distraction from the otherwise stressful journey.

"In America we call that part of the car a trunk," Bernadette said, laughing hysterically.

"See, that is just confusing, we call it the boot."

"How do you call it a boot, when a boot is a kind of shoe?" Bernadette said.

"Hey, don't blame us, blame the British."

Kwesi was now gazing at Bernadette's perfect set of teeth, which she covered with her hand when she laughed. Melvin had faded into the background and it seemed as if they were alone. They found themselves in each other's orbit again, and every time their eyes met, an exhilarating feeling rushed through them, one that Bernadette tried to hide. She never doubted her loyalty to Melvin, but she welcomed Kwesi's subtle flirtation, which eased her mind from their present dilemma.

THE TAXI PULLED up to the whitewashed walls of Elmina Castle just as a group of Chinese tourists were returning to their bus, exasperated from the sweltering heat. Kwesi paid the taxi driver and a young tour guide rushed up to them. "Americano?"

Melvin was about to answer when Kwesi interjected in Fanti, "I'm from here, just like you, so don't try it." He turned to Melvin and whispered, "He will charge you double if you say you are American." Melvin nodded, knowing Kwesi was right.

The tour guide handed them a brochure with a brief history of the castle:

It all started with the newly crowned Portuguese king, João II, in 1482. He wanted a permanent trading post in the Gulf of Guinea, so he ordered the castle prefabricated in Portugal and shipped on ten caravels along with provisions for six hundred men.

The tour guide pointed across the horizon. "You see that area over there?" Kwesi, Melvin, and Bernadette squinted to see what he was pointing at.

"That is where the Fanti chiefs rejected the Portuguese king's offer. They returned his rum, silks, and muskets. This offended King João, so he ordered his men to burn down their village."

The entire Fanti territory was torched, clearing the path for the massive project. It took six months to complete the castle, which was named Castelo de São Jorge da Mina. It was used primarily as a gold trading post until the Dutch captured it in 1642, turning it into the biggest slave trading center in West Africa.

Bernadette winced as the tour guide led them into a dark dungeon. The solitary light that seeped through a tiny hole conjured an eerie atmosphere. Melvin held his arm to his nose, gasping from the acrid air. "This is where the most rebellious enslaved Africans were kept," the tour guide said before leading them through a narrow tunnel that opened into an archway overlooking the sea. "And this is the door of no return," he said solemnly.

Bernadette's gaze was fixed on an etching on the dungeon walls. She walked closer and her heart skipped when she recognized the motif of a mermaid. She had seen that exact totem before. Her grandmother Ma' Susan had left it on her death-bed. Bernadette heard the clanging of iron chains against the stone walls and suddenly felt light-headed. Kwesi noticed. "I think we should go up." Melvin had begun to feel nauseated, so he didn't object. When they were aboveground, he turned to Bernadette. "Babe, you okay?" She nodded, offering a faint smile. Melvin could feel his stomach turning and he excused himself to the lavatory. Bernadette, alone with Kwesi, leaned against a giant cannon pointed toward the ocean. She stared into the vast emptiness. Kwesi reached for his Pentax camera and captured Bernadette, elegantly leaning against the cannon. He admitted to himself that she was the most beautiful woman he had ever seen. "So how did you meet the pastor?" Kwesi asked. Bernadette hesitated, her gaze still fixed on the undulating waves.

IT HAD BEEN three years since Ella departed for Philadelphia. Bernadette grew increasingly lonely, finding it difficult to make friends with the young waitresses Ray hired and fired routinely. To make things worse, most of the talented jazz musicians had ditched Baton Rouge for the more burgeoning scene in New Orleans. Ray, now a functional alcoholic, would stagger up to Bernadette when her shift was over. "El Ray's gonna be swinging again, Bern. Just wait and see."

"I believe you, Ray. I believe you," Bernadette would shout as she stepped into the predawn light, rushing home to care for Ma' Susan.

The aromatic smell of eucalyptus always welcomed Bernadette home in the morning. It was Ma' Susan's therapeutic treatment for her swollen legs that had left her mostly immobile. But no matter how much pain she was in, the sight of Bernadette always made her smile.

"My water baby home?"

"Yes, Ma," Bernadette would say as she massaged Ma' Susan's feet. That was her routine: late nights at El Ray's Jazz Club and early mornings at Ma' Susan's bedside. The only real excitement in Bernadette's life was when the mailman slid a white envelope with a Philadelphia stamp into their mailbox. She would run up to her room and inhale deeply before opening the envelope that contained Ella's letter. Their correspondence had been ongoing since Ella left for Philadelphia, and Bernadette knew every intricate detail of her life. Her difficult assimilation into the strict world of Villa Maria Catholic College. Her decision to study nursing against her parents' will, the obvious lack of boys at a women's Catholic college, and her plans to stay in Philadelphia after graduation. Bernadette replied to every one of Ella's letters, updating her on the comings and goings in Baton Rouge. Who got knocked up, who died, and who was getting married. Their correspondence went on uninterrupted for two years, and then the letters started coming less frequently and then not at all. The silence filled Bernadette with melancholy. She decided that as soon as she got the chance, she would go to Philadelphia and reunite with her best friend. Bernadette prayed to God for a sign, and it came one Saturday afternoon in the form of fire and brimstone.

Bernadette arrived at the Gus Young Avenue bus stop that morning and the smell of ashes lingered heavily in the air. She was surprised to find that a rubble of charred bricks had replaced the majestic façade of El Ray's Jazz Club. That was when she heard a familiar voice yelling, "I ain't do it. I swear to God, I ain't do it."

It was Ray, disheveled and handcuffed while screaming

from the back of a police squad car. Bernadette would later read in the newspapers that Ray Riboud, aka Manny Mankiewicz, aka Francis Favreau, and several other aka's she couldn't care to remember, had burned down his own club in an attempt to collect the insurance money. Bernadette was further spun out of her wits when she arrived home and the smell of eucalyptus was no longer in the air.

MA' SUSAN KNEW it was her time to go when she woke up that morning. She reached for the ornate photo album on her nightstand and ran her withered fingers across the images. Each photograph conjured a memory. Some painful, others heartwarming. Then she scribbled a note addressed to Bernadette:

> *My Water Baby.*
> *You have a purpose.*
> *Find it.*
> *Love, Grand Ma.*

Ma' Susan reached for a miniature totem of a mermaid she kept under her mattress. She kissed it and placed it gently on her note. Then she combed her gray hair, wore her most elegant dress, and played her favorite Billie Holiday album.

When Bernadette returned home, she heard the crackle of the gramophone and knew right then that Ma' Susan was gone. Bernadette read her note and sobbed inconsolably until the Baton Rouge Coroner's Office arrived.

MA' SUSAN'S FUNERAL was a somber event. Bernadette, along with members of the Calvary Baptist Church, listened to Reverend Bordelon as he delivered the eulogy. A solemn wake followed at the shotgun house that night. The guests took turns sharing stories of the woman who was beloved in her community. Aunt Mercy, Ma' Susan's best friend, served bowls of crawfish gumbo and home-brewed beer. The wake lasted deep into the night, and Bernadette sobbed with each new Ma' Susan story she heard. The emptiness that followed Ma' Susan's home-going was too much for Bernadette. She put up the shotgun house for sale and began her journey to Philadelphia, in search of her best friend, Ella.

THE BUS RIDE to Philadelphia took almost twenty hours, with brief restroom stops along the way. When Bernadette finally arrived at the Penn Station bus depot, she was famished. She had neglected to eat the sandwiches that sat squished between her favorite cardigan and her cosmetics box. Armed only with a stack of letters, Bernadette inquired about the address atop Ella's envelopes.

"Excuse me, ma'am, can you—"

The woman just brushed past Bernadette without acknowledging her.

"Excuse me, sir, do you—"

The man quickened his pace without even glancing at her.

For nearly half an hour Bernadette tried to find someone, anyone, who could tell her where she could find 2335 Snyder Avenue. But everyone in the large bus terminal seemed in such a hurry. Mothers dragging their snotty-nosed kids behind them. Reunited lovers entangled in hugs. The discordant sounds of grinding pistons and idle bus engines were only made worse by a rowdy group of newspaper boys harassing passengers.

"Extra, extra. Read all about it," they shouted.

"JFK orders embargo on all Cuban goods."

Bernadette finally spotted a Negro police officer standing next to the ticket booth, and she hurried toward him. "You will have to catch the Green Line trolley, madam," the officer said, after reading the address on the envelope. Then he pointed at a long line of passengers waiting outside the station. "Tell the operator you are going to Snyder Avenue." Bernadette smiled, admiring the officer's sharp navy-blue uniform and shiny gold buttons that glistened in the sun.

"Thank you, sir," Bernadette said, grabbing her suitcase.

The trolley was overflowing with passengers, stumbling and grabbing each other whenever the operator made an abrupt stop. The sun was in its final throes, and it cast a splendid hue over the entire city. Bernadette paid her fare and disembarked at the Snyder Avenue stop. She walked along the exquisite row homes that lined the street. Then she came to a burgundy two-story house with a white fenced gate. The numbers 2335 hung neatly on the door. Bernadette suddenly got cold feet. What in God's name was she thinking? Showing up unannounced at what she hoped was Ella's doorstep? Bernadette considered finding a hostel for the night instead, but the dark clouds had swallowed whatever remained of the sun, and so, reluctantly, she knocked—faintly.

A man who looked to be in his thirties cracked the door open. His Afro was unkempt and he sported an equally disheveled goatee. He held a baby over his shoulder and patted him gently. "May I help you?"

Bernadette adjusted her dress. "Good evening, sir, does Ella Turner live here?"

"Ella? Yes, that's my wife."

Wife? Bernadette almost said, but she kept her composure. "Is she home?"

"Yes, of course. Come in."

Bernadette grabbed her suitcase and stepped into the large living room, which was decorated with a set of pastel-colored furniture, punctuated by a large oak center table. Bernadette glanced around the room until she landed on a photograph of Ella performing at El Ray's. A voice seeped out of the kitchen.

"Honey, I told you to keep the window closed, the baby is—"

Ella stopped short. Her jaw dropped and her eyes widened.

"BERNADETTE? IS THAT YOU?" she yelled, as she rushed and hugged Bernadette, clasping her so tight that she could have suffocated her.

"Ella, I missed you," Bernadette said in a muffled voice, eyes misty.

Ella's husband returned with a glass of water in one hand and the sleeping baby in his other arm.

"I see you met Kareem and Junior," Ella said as she slumped into the couch next to Bernadette.

"So this is the Bernadette I've heard so much about?" Kareem said as he handed Bernadette the glass. "It's great to finally put a face to the name."

Bernadette blushed as she drank the water in huge gulps. From the corner of her eye she caught a glimpse of a wedding portrait. It was Ella dressed in a Muslim hijab and Kareem wearing a kufi, smiling lovingly.

"How old is he?" Bernadette asked, trying to distract herself from the photograph.

"Eleven months," both Ella and Kareem responded, at the same time, in a staggered chorus. Then Kareem, realizing his presence was wearing thin, said, "I'll go put the baby down and let you ladies catch up. May Allah be praised."

"Thanks, honey," Ella responded as he disappeared into the bedroom.

"I'm so happy to see you, Bern. I know it's been a while since I wrote. But life happens, you know."

"You don't have to apologize," Bernadette said.

"Kareem is a good man," Ella sniveled, wiping her moist cheeks with the back of her hand.

"So you Mooslim now?" Bernadette chuckled.

"I sure is," Ella replied.

"Tell me you still performing."

"Girl, I ain't hit the stage since I left Baton Rouge. Besides, look at me now."

Ella gestured at her flabby arm.

"I bet you can still sing circles around them skinny heifers."

Both women burst into a laughing fit that lasted for a while. Bernadette told Ella about Ray burning down his own club, and they reminisced about him literally shitting on the competition. After hours of laughter, Ella led Bernadette to a small bedroom. "We set up the space for Junior, but he still sleeps with us. You're welcome to stay as long as you want."

Bernadette took Ella up on her offer and stayed at their beautiful home on Snyder Avenue. But the inevitable collision of familiarity and contempt soon got the best of her. Seeing Ella happily married and raising a child was too much for Bernadette. Once again, she wished she had what Ella had.

To make things worse, Bernadette suffered a severe case of writer's block, forcing her to abandon the novel she had begun to write. It was the one thing from her past she was determined to continue, but grief had clouded any creative spark she'd wished for.

In search of inspiration, she found an apartment on Tasker Street, atop a local bookstore owned by Mr. Lomax. He hired Bernadette as his assistant and she instantly fell in love with her job. She would disappear into the pages and prose of the masterpieces stacked on the dusty shelves. Brilliant Negro writers like Richard Wright, Claude McKay, Pauline Hopkins, all captivated Bernadette. Occasionally, she would assist a customer or two, suggesting new titles or timeless classics.

One morning after haggling with Mr. Lomax over the price of a first-edition copy of Ralph Ellison's *Invisible Man*, Bernadette returned to stacking a delivery of books when a sharply dressed man stepped inside.

"Good day," the gentleman said, tipping his hat in Mr. Lomax's direction. "Got any automobile catalogs?"

Mr. Lomax kept his eyes fixed on his crossword puzzle.

"Bern, we got a customer," he yelled.

Bernadette stepped out from behind the bookshelf. Her eyes met the gentleman's and she froze, taking him in. He was tall, handsome, and reminded her of a Negro movie star whose name she couldn't remember.

"I said we got a customer." Mr. Lomax glanced at Bernadette, then to the gentleman, whose eyes were locked on Bernadette. "Y'all know each other or summin'?"

"No, sir," Bernadette finally said.

The gentleman quickly removed his hat. "I'm—I'm looking for a catalog—automobile catalog."

"We have a few in the back," Bernadette said, leading him

through a maze of bookshelves. "These are our newest ones, sir."

"It's Melvin—you can call me Mel."

He held his hand out and when Bernadette reached out to shake it, Melvin cupped her hand between both of his. She felt a sensation she had never experienced before. Tongue-tied, she mumbled, "Bern. My name is Bern."

"I hope I don't embarrass you by saying this, but you are the most beautiful woman I ever seen. I mean that sincerely," Melvin said while slowly freeing her hand.

Bernadette wished she could conjure something witty in response, but she failed to find the words. So instead she mustered a coy smile. "Why, thank you. You ain't half bad-looking either."

Melvin started to burst out laughing but caught it in the palm of his hand. "Half bad-looking?"

"You know what I mean," Bernadette replied as she handed Melvin one of the catalogs. He went for her hand again, but she quickly dodged while laughing. It had only been two minutes since he walked through the door, but something about Melvin was spellbinding, and Bernadette allowed herself to be captivated by his charm. The only thing she regretted was not wearing her more alluring dress she'd glanced at while perusing her closet that morning.

Mr. Lomax, beginning to suspect something was amiss, adjusted his rimless glasses and cleared his throat, loud enough to interrupt their blissful encounter. Bernadette ducked behind the large bookshelf, just out of Mr. Lomax's view. She beamed, relishing the mischievous thrill of infatuation, one she hadn't experienced in a while.

She raised her finger to her lips and whispered, "You gonna get me fired, mister."

"I wouldn't wanna do that." Melvin smiled and flipped through the April issue of *American Automobile*. He nodded gracefully and waltzed to the cash register, where Mr. Lomax was leaning capriciously.

"That all you need?"

"Yes, sir," Melvin said, glancing at Bernadette. "Nice to make your acquaintance, ma'am," he said as he strolled out the door.

Bernadette's heart sank. He'd not asked for her number and there'd been no time to slip him hers. What if she never saw him again? This spark was unlike anything she'd ever felt.

So she grabbed her jacket and hurried up to Mr. Lomax.

"I'm gonna take my lunch now, sir."

Mr. Lomax glanced at his watch and frowned. "Lunch at ten A.M.?"

"Well, I'm hungry now," Bernadette said, halfway out the door.

"Yep, I bet you are," Mr. Lomax replied sarcastically.

BERNADETTE STEPPED ONTO Tasker Street, eyes frantically searching for a man in a sharp gray suit and black fedora. *Dammit,* she thought to herself. She'd really let him get away. Then a voice stopped her.

"You looking for someone?"

Bernadette turned swiftly to see Melvin gazing at her. She wanted to run up and hug him, but that would be unladylike. So she shook her head nonchalantly. "I just came out for some air. What you still doing here?"

"I was gonna wait out here all day if I had to, just for the chance to see you again."

Bernadette blushed. "Well, ain't no sense in just standing here. It's a beautiful day, and the park is usually empty around this time."

Melvin and Bernadette found a bench in Columbus Park facing a small pond. A chorus of croaks echoed from the frogs that leapt on the lily pads, occasionally splashing out of the murky water.

"I ain't never seen no Negro buy this here catalog," Bernadette said, flipping through the vibrant pages of vehicles.

"That's because no Negro owns a dealership in South Philly. Been saving up for that. I'm gonna be the first."

"Oh, really?" Bernadette said, admiring Melvin's bravado.

"Your boss sure is hawkish," he continued. "You like working there?"

"Yeah, it pays the bills, but it's also the inspiration I've been needing to write."

"You a writer?"

Bernadette nodded with a shy grin.

"Ain't that something. I bet you write as gorgeously as you look."

"I'm okay, still finding my voice, you know."

"Got anything I can read?"

"Well, I'm in the early stages of something."

"Can you tell me what it's about?"

"It's still a rough idea, but it's called 'The Secret of the Bayou.'" Bernadette's eyes lit up, excited to share her story. "It's about a woman who goes back in time to save her lover."

"That sounds romantic." Melvin smiled.

"I'm still trying to work out the character conflicts, but I'm real close."

"Well, I promise I'ma read it when it's done."

Bernadette looked into Melvin's eyes; it was all happening so fast, her caution dissipating, yet she didn't resist. On that park bench, on that beautiful morning, Melvin picked up the courage to ask Bernadette out, and their passionate romance began.

Bernadette had finally found what she'd been looking for: the chance to have a family of her own. On quiet nights, they strolled hand in hand through the empty lot in Germantown. "This gonna change our lives, Bern," Melvin would say as he gave Bernadette an exquisite imaginary tour of his dream car dealership. They had found in each other a believer, and it seemed nothing could tear them apart.

THE SHUTTER OF Kwesi's camera interrupted Bernadette's reverie.

"What did you say?"

"I asked how you met the pastor?"

"Oh, church. I met Melvin at church," Bernadette said, averting her eyes.

The last group of Chinese tourists were leaving the castle when Melvin returned from the lavatory. He looked scruffy and his eyes were bloodshot. Melvin didn't expect his first adventure on the way to Nkrumah to be so harrowing.

"Is there a place around here we can get a drink?" he asked.

"Pastor, are you sure?" Kwesi replied, surprised.

Melvin smiled and rolled up his sleeves. "Jesus turned water into wine, didn't he?"

. . .

IT WAS LATE in the evening when Melvin, Bernadette, and Kwesi arrived at the bar. It had a seedy façade with no signage and squalid furniture. Melvin didn't care about its ramshackle state. He desperately needed a drink and this place was as good as any.

The proprietress instantly recognized Kwesi. When "Mami Wata Highlife" blared out of the speakers, she offered him and his guests extra drinks on the house. Kwesi turned to Melvin and Bernadette. "I hope you are enjoying the real Ghana."

Melvin chuckled, watching the couples sway on the dance floor. Bernadette was back in a good mood and wanted to dance too.

"Just one song," she whispered to Melvin. He considered it, then shook his head. "Babe, I'm tired, plus this drink stronger than I thought."

Bernadette turned to Kwesi. "Can you teach me to dance the highlife?"

Kwesi, wide-eyed and ambivalent, glanced at Melvin.

"Don't let me stop you," Melvin said, now wishing he had said yes to Bernadette.

King Bruce and the Black Beats' song "Baby Juli Yaba" rattled the aluminum roof as Kwesi held Bernadette in his arms. He tried to keep a respectable gap of space between them, arms wide, shoulders and pelvis arched. He occasionally glanced at Melvin, who just kept throwing back one shot after the other, doing his best to ignore them. Kwesi remained cautious, keeping his hands above Bernadette's waist. She noticed he was rigid and less graceful than the other men.

"Relax, Kwesi," she whispered. "It's just a dance."

But the more Kwesi danced, the more nervous he got. So he stepped back warily. "We have an early departure to Kulungugu tomorrow. We better get going."

ON THE RIDE back, Melvin rested his head on Bernadette's shoulder, snoring loudly. There was a comfortable silence between Kwesi and Bernadette. The taxi pulled up to the hotel and Bernadette turned to Kwesi. "Thank you for everything."

He nodded politely. "See you in the morning."

WHEN BERNADETTE FINALLY got Melvin in bed, she reminded herself that this wasn't a vacation, and she was far from a tourist. The FBI was still on their trail and she needed to remain vigilant. Kwesi's attraction to her could be a useful cover, she thought. It would temper his curiosity and blur any inconsistencies in their story. Then, as she considered their use of Kwesi, she wondered if he too could harbor ulterior motives. Why was he so quick to allow them to join the journey? She had read stories about foreigners using Americans for visas in search of the supposed American dream, but Kwesi's actions seemed motivated by a genuine interest in her, and nothing more.

THAT NIGHT, MELVIN tossed and turned in bed, haunted by a dream so vivid it plagued him the entire next day. He was back in his childhood home in Virginia, although it looked smaller than he remembered. As he opened the living room door it transformed into an endless haunting void. A bright oscillating light blinded him briefly, and he realized that he was back at Mr. Moretti's sawmill. He saw his father prostrated on a gurney. He was laughing at something underneath the cot. When Melvin lowered his gaze, he saw Mr. Moretti in the form of a wildebeest, licking the blood from Melvin's father's amputated arm. Mr. Moretti suddenly stopped and growled at Melvin. His glimmering eyes burned with malice. Without warning, Mr. Moretti pounced on Melvin, ripping his arm with his sharp claws.

Melvin gasped and jolted awake. He wiped the sweat from his brow, breathing heavily. Then he froze, realizing Bernadette wasn't in bed with him. Melvin rushed toward the bathroom. When he pushed in the door, he saw Bernadette submerged in the bathtub, overflowing with water. She looked pale, as though she'd been in there for hours, perhaps even drowned. Melvin panicked and shook her limp body. Bernadette's eyes popped open and she splashed out of the tub.

"Babe, you scared me," Melvin quavered.

CHAPTER 5

Kwesi was leaning against the tour bus when Melvin and Bernadette stepped out of the hotel lobby. He extinguished his cigarette between his fingers and smiled brightly. "Good morning, Kwesi." Bernadette returned his smile as she handed her suitcase to a stiff and fractious Melvin. He stacked their bags between the band equipment, jerry cans of water, and a small provisions box. Bernadette admired the beige Bluebird bus with an immaculate hand-painted sign: *KWESI KWAYSON & HIS DYNAMO BAND*.

The bus was Kwesi's only valuable possession after his record label representative stole his royalties and fled Ghana. That was a typical record label racket, and DecArt Records was no different. Their Africa representative was a long-haired hippie named Ian Hemings. Ian lived in the pubs and brothels of London before he was sent to Ghana to discover a highlife artist the label could sign. He traveled for months, visiting every hole-in-the-wall club and palm wine bar, hoping to find a sensational Ghanaian act. His truck was retrofitted with a portable recording studio in the back. He cut a record in each village he visited, but his bosses in London were un-impressed with the demos he sent.

One night, as Ian was driving back to Accra, he heard a new singer on the radio called Kwesi Kwayson. Ian was so blown away that he waited outside the Ghana Broadcasting Corporation until Kwesi and his band finished their live session. Ian offered Kwesi a record contract on the spot. A few days later, they cut a five-song album with the lead single "Mami Wata Highlife." Ian's bosses in London were ecstatic and gave Kwesi an advance of £200, enough to buy a tour bus. "Mami Wata Highlife" became an international hit, earning Kwesi over £10,000 in royalties, a fortune no local musician had ever earned. But when Kwesi went to the DecArt Records office in Accra to collect his royalty payment, he discovered the hard truth. Ian had absconded with his money and was back in the pubs and brothels of London. Kwesi was lucky to have purchased a tour bus with his advance because he never saw another penny from the album.

MELVIN AND BERNADETTE climbed aboard the bus exchanging lukewarm hellos with the three men seated in the back. "Let me introduce you," Kwesi said.

"That's Ato, my driver, and tour manager." Ato paused checking the speedometer and shook Melvin's and Bernadette's hands. "Akwaaba," he said buoyantly.

Kwesi continued, "That's T, the drummer, and that's Panyin, the guitarist, and that's Kakra, the bassist." Panyin and Kakra were identical twins and although they had toured with Kwesi for almost a year, he still confused the two.

"No, I'm Panyin," one of them said, "and he's Kakra."

Kwesi, mortified by the mistake, apologized. The only person who remained silent was T, the drummer. He just twirled his drumsticks and shrugged. Kwesi gestured. "That's Bernadette, and that's Pastor. They are American missionaries and will be traveling with us to Kulungugu."

T sucked his teeth. "Missionaries? I don't believe it." He chuckled.

Melvin frowned, perturbed at how easily T saw through them. That was T's nature. He had a special gift for getting under people's skin. It could have been his short, stocky frame, his shimmering bald head, or the distinguishing tribal marks that cut across his face. Whatever the reason, T had a confrontational spirit and he clashed with almost everybody. It was also the reason Kwesi had fired him twice. On both occasions, he returned because something tragic happened to his replacement. The first drummer broke his arm in a local football game. The second fractured his hip in a motorbike accident. Some people suspected that T was behind both incidents, but they couldn't prove it. Besides being a malcontent, T was also a philanderer. His antics almost got the band killed in Nigeria, but few people knew the details of that story.

IT WAS THE West African leg of the Mami Wata tour, and Lagos was their last stop. That night, the line at the Yaba Night Club wrapped around the building twice. The euphoric crowd requested "Mami Wata Highlife" fifteen times in a row. A new record, from Abidjan's eleven requests. It didn't matter that the cheap generator fluttered to a halt midway through the show. The energy was rapturous. Soon, the band was swarmed by gorgeous Lagos women looking for a good time.

It was all going well until Kwesi heard the chanting of a cutlass-wielding mob rushing to their hotel.

It turned out that one of the women T brought back to his room was the wife of a powerful oilman. He organized the area boys and they came for blood. T narrowly escaped by jumping out of the third-floor window and hiding behind the hotel wall. When Kwesi and the band pulled up in the bus, they were surprised to find T, buck naked with a pair of leaves covering his private parts. The oilman collapsed when they broke into T's room and found his wife in bed with another woman. His goons chased the tour bus on motorbikes, and just when Kwesi thought they had lost them, one of the bikers aimed a shotgun and fired through their back window. Ato swerved the wheel just as the bullet shattered the glass. It grazed the seat and tore through the dashboard. T, who had narrowly escaped the mob, realized that the leaves covering his private parts were, in fact, poison ivy. Needless to say, the itch was unbearable. To make things worse, Kwesi, Ato, and the twins were so enraged by T's recklessness that they threw him off the bus when they arrived at the Ghana border to teach him a lesson. It took T two whole days to hitchhike back to Cape Coast, a near impossible task for a buck-naked man. Since then, T maintained a hostile attitude toward everyone, and Melvin and Bernadette were no different.

THE BUS MANEUVERED slowly through a cluster of potholes. Bernadette leaned against the window with her chin propped in her hand. She gazed at the desolate road ahead, awestruck by the famished blades of savanna grass that lined the horizon. Melvin, still in a funk, tried to banish the baleful images from his wildebeest dream. He hadn't thought about Mr. Moretti in years. The dream unearthed a labyrinth of resentment that Melvin tried to forget.

They had been driving for two hours and Kwesi, T, and the twins dozed off.

As the bus sped down an incline, Ato slammed on the brakes, jolting everyone awake. Kwesi wiped the sleep from his eyes and saw a military roadblock ahead. He glanced at Melvin and Bernadette. "Please have your passports ready."

Melvin's heart sank and Bernadette trembled as they pretended to dig through their bags for the passports. A blue Peugeot ahead of them was flagged to the side of the road by two Kalashnikov-wielding soldiers. A man dressed in a tan suit stepped out of the Peugeot and popped his trunk. Melvin remembered the .38-caliber Ruger stashed in his shoulder bag. "Fuck," he murmured to himself. He had planned to dump the gun before they departed, but it slipped his mind. Suddenly, one of the soldiers swung a lightning-fast punch, striking the jaw of the man wearing the tan suit. "Jesus," a chorus rang out in the bus. Everyone sat up to see what was happening. The second officer slammed his rifle butt into the man's face, sending him crashing to the asphalt. Ato, now alarmed, frantically searched his pockets for his driver's license. The soldiers dragged the unconscious man to the army truck, handcuffed him, and motioned Ato to the side of the road. As the bus eased to a stop, Kwesi turned to everyone. "Please, let me do the talking."

The soldier stuck his head in the driver's window and darted his eyes around sharply from underneath his oversized helmet. "Identification," he scoffed.

Melvin was about to tell him that their passports were

missing, when the second soldier yelled, "Kwesi Kwayson and His Dynamo Band? Ebi you that?"

Kwesi smiled, finally at ease. "Ebi me oh."

The other soldier rushed to Kwesi's side of the bus, neglecting to check any identification. Melvin and Bernadette exhaled, temporarily relieved.

"What you dey do for here?" the soldier asked.

"We dey go play show for President Nkrumah," Kwesi replied.

"You for make careful. The coup plotters dey road top." The soldier pointed at the unconscious man handcuffed to the army truck.

"We just arrest one of the men wey kill Sergeant Asare."

"Sergeant Asare?"

Bernadette glanced at Melvin, remembering that she never told him about Sergeant Asare's death in the newspaper. Kwesi thanked the soldiers with a signed copy of "Mami Wata Highlife" on 45-RPM vinyl. The bus pulled off in a spray of gravel as the soldiers waved goodbye.

THE PARCHED SAVANNA grass gave way to a lush verdant forest with a single-lane road cutting through it. Ato, yawning behind the wheel, switched on the radio to keep from dozing off. He turned the dial and a loud static sound reverberated. The bullet fired by the Nigerian biker was still lodged in the dashboard and occasionally interfered with the radio transmission. Ato fidgeted with the dial until he got a clean signal. An advertisement for Star beer buzzed through, and when he turned the dial again, the unmistakable voice of Aretha Franklin seeped out of the speakers. Ato was about to turn the dial when Melvin blurted, "Please, leave it on." Melvin was surprised to hear the melancholic melody of "One Step Ahead" on Ghanaian radio. It took him back to the last time he'd heard it.

IT WAS THE twenty-sixth of December, 1965, the fateful night that triggered an avalanche of events that turned Melvin and Bernadette into fugitives. But the day began like any other, with Melvin, slung low behind the wheel of his brand-new Chevrolet Impala, cruising down the 85 freeway toward Alabama. The sleek dashboard with fine silver detailing reflected Bernadette's soft features as she slept with her head resting on the leather seat. This had become their weekend routine, a thirteen-hour drive to Alabama. They visited used-car auctions, where Melvin intended to buy a small fleet for his dealership. Melvin and Bernadette also volunteered at the Alabama State University branch of SNCC, where they helped train nonviolent student protesters. They had become increasingly active in the civil rights movement in Philadelphia, and their trips to Alabama put them in the epicenter of the struggle.

THE SIX O'CLOCK news bulletin rattled the Chevy's speakers, and it finally dawned on Melvin that they hadn't seen a single open restaurant for miles. Bernadette woke up fatigued and famished. It had been seven hours since they last ate the leftovers from their Christmas dinner. "Pass me the book, babe," Melvin said, flicking his cigarette out the window. Bernadette popped the glove compartment and grabbed the *Green Book,* also known as the Negro motorist's bible. It cataloged all Negro-owned and Negro-friendly restaurants, hotels, and gas stations that were safe to patronize. Melvin's face collapsed when he realized they had already driven past the last restaurant in the area.

"We could just wait till we get to the auction to eat," Bernadette said, sliding the *Green Book* back into the glove compartment.

"Yeah, sure, we could just wait," Melvin replied in a defeated tone.

THE NIGHT SKY had swallowed the last remnants of twilight when the Chevrolet Impala pulled into Auburn, Alabama. A light drizzle moistened the windshield, and Melvin occasionally flicked the wiper control to clear his view.

Bernadette, still starving, decided to get some shut-eye. The only company Melvin had was Aretha Franklin's "One Step Ahead" pouring out of the radio. Melvin had heard the song several times, but he had never paid attention to the lyrics. But on that wet December night, he felt the blues when Aretha sang:

I'm only one step ahead of heartbreak,
One step ahead of misery.

Melvin saw the hazy lights of a diner ahead. Against his better judgment he pulled into the parking lot. His eyes cut across the large windows, scanning for patrons. When he was satisfied that they were alone, Melvin tapped Bernadette's shoulder gently. "Wake up, babe, we can try to get some food here."

She was too sleepy to protest, so she just mumbled, "Thanks, Mel."

Melvin threw his coat over Bernadette to shield her from the pelting rain as they hurried toward the blinking *OTTO'S DINER* neon sign.

A large freckle-faced white woman smiled pleasantly when Melvin and Bernadette walked in, and they exhaled a sigh of relief.

"Merry Christmas. Y'all can sit wherever ya want," she said, filling a pitcher with water.

Melvin, reassured by the amiable welcome, loosened his posture and led Bernadette to a table tucked against a large window. It overlooked the parking lot, so Melvin figured if there was a fuss, they would have an advantage. They were scanning through the menu when a tall man with a gaunt face stepped out of the kitchen. He wiped his hands on his apron and dug out a pad. "Hi, I am Otto. You having what?"

Melvin gestured to Bernadette. "I'll have the baked chicken with mashed potatoes," she said. Otto scribbled it down and turned to Melvin. "And for you?"

"Same," Melvin answered, closing the menu.

"Danke schön," Otto blurted, and strolled back to the kitchen.

Hearing Otto's thick accent reminded Melvin of his time in Germany during the war.

MELVIN HAD NEVER thought of enlisting in the army. But after he dropped out of Lincoln University, he couldn't find any work. The only jobs readily available to Negroes were at the steel mills in Pittsburgh, which Melvin abhorred. He decided that he would start his own used-car business. He found an open lot in Germantown and negotiated a down payment.

But when Melvin went to the bank to inquire about a loan, he was rudely escorted out.

That was when he heard President Roosevelt's radio broadcast encouraging Negroes to join the war effort in Germany. Melvin packed his few belongings and was soon heading to Fort Huachuca in Arizona.

Basic training took four weeks and Melvin became one of the first Negro soldiers to see ground combat in Würzburg, Germany. His infantry unit overran a Nazi stronghold, capturing over two thousand prisoners of war.

So, as Melvin sat in Otto's Diner, he couldn't help but see the irony of it all. Otto, who was most likely an enemy combatant, could migrate to America, start a new life, and open a restaurant in Alabama, where a Negro who fought for America was scared to eat.

THE SOUND OF silverware snapped Melvin back to himself. Otto served two plates of baked chicken and the aroma swept through the diner.

"I went to look at the dress yesterday," Bernadette said, flooding her mashed potatoes with gravy. "I think you're gonna like it, Mel, it ain't like the other wedding gowns we seen."

Melvin smiled, enchanted by his bride-to-be. "I know you're gonna look beautiful, Bern." Melvin's mind drifted to the church where they planned to tie the knot. Then suddenly a smashing sound startled him. He turned to see a group of shadowy white men surrounding his Chevrolet Impala. One of the men swung a large baseball bat at the windshield, shattering it on impact. Bernadette stared out the window, horrified. Then Melvin leapt up, eyes burning with rage. He brushed past Otto, who shouted, "Bitte hör auf. No go outside please. I call police for you."

But it was too late. Melvin had already stormed out with Bernadette giving chase, yelling for him to stop, to stay in. The men surrounded Melvin, seething and sinister. They all wielded bats except the man with a large beard, who aimed a Colt .45 pistol at Melvin. The man who appeared to be the ringleader wore a sleeveless shirt. "What ya doin' round here, boy?" he sneered, grabbing Bernadette by her blouse. "Whatchu say we take her out back and show her a good time?" The men burst out laughing, showing a variety of discolored teeth and porous gums.

Melvin remembered what he had learned in basic training. The art of disarming an enemy combatant. A swift set of moves that had saved his life in Germany. Suddenly he twisted the man's arm, snatched the gun, and pulled the trigger.

The man in the sleeveless shirt crashed to the ground, blood gushing out of his skull. Melvin pointed the pistol at the other men and they bolted in different directions. Bernadette, dazed, walked over to Melvin and hugged him. Otto came running out of the diner. "Scheisse, Scheisse, you must go now. They hang you, if they catch you."

Melvin nodded, stuck the Colt .45 pistol in his pocket, and cleared the broken glass off the Impala's seats. As they pulled out of Otto's parking lot, tears flooded Bernadette's eyes. Melvin, starting to grapple with their situation, turned to her and said the words he would repeat several times again. "It'll all work out, babe, I promise."

CHAPTER 6

The humidity had worsened when the bus pulled into Akosombo, after six hours on the road. Everyone except Kwesi and Ato had succumbed to the exhaustion. They decided to spend the night in town, so they pulled into an AGIP petrol station that stood adjacent to the Akosombo hydroelectric dam.

Half a dozen Russian soldiers armed with Kalashnikov rifles were guarding the main gate. Melvin and Bernadette concealed their apprehension as they drove past a Soviet GAZ Chaika vehicle parked in the lot.

"Those Russians have been here for months," Kwesi said as he opened the station door.

"Why are they here?" Bernadette asked.

"Nkrumah is afraid that the Americans will sabotage the dam, so he sent them to protect it." Melvin followed closely behind Kwesi, eavesdropping on the story he told Bernadette about how Nkrumah became America's nemesis.

"IT ALL STARTED when Nkrumah was sworn in as president. He was trying to industrialize Ghana quickly, and he knew cheap electricity was the best way to do it."

. . .

PRESIDENT NKRUMAH COMMISSIONED an inquiry into building a hydroelectric dam on the Volta Lake. His detractors argued that the cost of the dam would be perilous to newly independent Ghana, and, in fact, it was.

"That was Nkrumah's first mistake," Kwesi said, perusing the scant provisions on the shelf. "He borrowed two hundred million dollars from the Americans. Can you believe that?"

After the construction of the dam, the Americans accused Nkrumah of becoming heavily influenced by the Russians. He was branded a communist and the Americans backed out of the agreement.

"That is why they want to assassinate him," Kwesi said. "They have tried at least two times with the coup plotters. Some people say the SSV are the only reason he is still alive."

"The SSV?" Bernadette asked, baffled.

"Yes, the SSV. I forget what it stands for—shape shifters something. They are soldiers who can transform into different animals. Anyway, that is why there are Russian soldiers protecting the—"

The sound of a bottle opener interrupted Kwesi's story. The young clerk behind the counter passed him three Coca-Cola bottles. "Sorry the Coke is warm, sah. No electricity," the clerk said in a dismal tone.

Kwesi, sensing the tension between Melvin and Bernadette, handed them their bottles and excused himself. They stood under the AGIP store awning, which cast a shadow across the parking lot. Bernadette took Melvin's hand gently. "I know you don't like Kwesi, Mel, but we need him to get to the president, you know that."

Melvin's eyes were fixed on T, who was talking on the station telephone in a low tone. His secretive demeanor made Melvin nervous. Had T discovered that they were fugitives? Was he calling to alert the police?

"Mel, you heard what I said?" Bernadette asked.

"Who said I don't like Kwesi?" Melvin finally replied.

"I see the way you act when he is around."

"The way I act? Have you seen how you act?" Melvin chugged the bottle of Coke, suddenly stopping to spit it all out. "Who the fuck buys warm Coke anyway?"

A GROUP OF Russian soldiers pulled up to the AGIP station in a KamAZ tactical vehicle. They stumbled out, taking swigs from a vodka bottle, not a sober one among them. Melvin and Bernadette were heading back to the bus when a Russian soldier pointed at Melvin. "Comrades, it is actor Sidney Poitier."

Melvin shook his head vehemently. "Nope. I ain't Sidney Poitier."

"You are American actor Sidney Poitier, no?"

"Look, you may think all Negroes look alike, but I assure you, I'm not Sidney Poitier." Bernadette couldn't help but chuckle at the awkward Russians who continued to pester Melvin.

"My name Boris, I watch all movie with you. I see *Paris Blues*. You and Paul Newman. Illegal in Soviet Union, but we watch anyway."

"Nope, I said I ain't Sidney Poitier," Melvin muttered exasperatedly. Another Russian soldier shook Melvin's hand vigorously. "You make new film in Ghana? You act as pastor?"

"No, I'm not making a film in Ghana and I'm not acting as a pastor." Melvin grabbed Bernadette's hand and attempted to push past the soldiers who blocked his path, stumbling over each other. Kwesi saw the commotion from the bus window and rushed out.

"Please make picture with Sidney Poitier," one of the Russian soldiers yelled when they saw Kwesi's camera.

Melvin, realizing the Russians wouldn't leave him alone until they got a picture, agreed reluctantly. "My name Boris, don't forget me," the young soldier whispered with his breath reeking of vodka. He joined the other soldiers squeezed between Melvin and Bernadette. Kwesi pointed the camera and with each shutter click, the Russians assumed a new pose, each one more ludicrous than the last. Finally, they handed Melvin a permanent marker and he autographed anything they could grab. Helmets, boots, cigarette packets. By the time Melvin was done, he had scribbled his fake Sidney Poitier signature a dozen times with the names Boris, Oleg, Dimitri, and Igor. The Russians offered to sing Melvin and Bernadette a Russian folk song, but before they could commence, the gregarious Boris puked his guts all over Oleg's boots, and a fight quickly ensued between the drunk soldiers. They tussled on the dusty pavement yelling obscenities in various Russian dialects.

"Stop now!" a command thundered. The voice was a mix of an eagle's shriek and a lion's roar. Bernadette's skin began to crawl. The Russian soldiers quickly rose to their feet. When Melvin, Bernadette, and Kwesi turned around, they saw a Ghanaian soldier staring at the Russians in disgust. His eyes gleamed, almost reptilian. The soldier wore a badge on his shoulder with the inscription *SSV*. "Get back to your base," he thundered again. The Russians quickly scurried to their tactical vehicle and sped off.

"I am sorry those men harassed you," the soldier said, his voice now sounding human. "They are having a difficult time in Ghana. Maybe it is the humidity, or the vodka, or both. They are slowly going mad."

Bernadette nodded, avoiding the soldier's eyes.

"We were just on our way," Kwesi stammered, nudging Melvin and Bernadette, who quickly followed him toward the bus, leaving the strange soldier alone under the station awning.

THE ORANGE HUES of sunset had swallowed the sky when Ato pulled into Akosombo Lodge. His weary passengers disembarked, dragging their luggage behind them. The lodge was a sturdy two-story structure, built in the late 1920s by famed Italian architect Benito Pigozzi. The thatched roof and lobby archway were a rare blend of traditional African and Western architecture. Bernadette was in awe of the large paintings that hung on the mud walls. They had been commissioned by the original owner, the British aristocrat and explorer Sir Richard Chamberlain.

Sir Richard had spent a fortune in Africa, searching for the elusive treasure that belonged to the twelfth-century ruler and onetime richest man in the world Mansa Musa. It is believed that Mansa Musa buried over a hundred thousand ounces of gold in modern-day Ghana, after his famed journey from ancient Mali to Mecca. Sir Richard hired renowned cartographers and spent a decade of his life searching for Mansa Musa's treasure. He eventually died of cholera, leaving behind the majestic building that became the Akosombo Lodge.

MELVIN AND BERNADETTE were relieved to learn that passports weren't necessary to check in. The apathetic young receptionist was, however, oblivious to his task. He mistakenly gave Kwesi and Bernadette a couples suite and handed Melvin a single room key. Kwesi instantly corrected him, but not before Melvin commented, "Oh, so you two are sharing a room now?" Bernadette rolled her eyes and the receptionist giggled mischievously.

"Sorry, Pastor, I didn't know you were with the lady, sah."

That evening, Kwesi, Melvin, and Bernadette ate dinner in the lodge cafeteria. It was a large room that overlooked the placid Volta Lake. The yam and spinach stew, perfectly simmered in a pot of palm oil, diffused a succulent aroma. Bernadette and Melvin both devoured their portions. After letting out a deep belch, Melvin, heavy-eyed, stood and beckoned Bernadette to follow. "I'll be up in a few," she said, as Melvin made his way to their room.

Kwesi and Bernadette sat in the quiet cafeteria gazing at the luminous fireflies rattling the windowsill. "I have to apologize for my fiancé, he gets cranky when he's tired."

"Cranky?"

"Yes, like irritated, or angry."

"Ah, I understand what you mean," Kwesi said. "You don't have to apologize. Ghana is hot and humid. Sometimes I get cranky too." Kwesi smiled, proud to add a new word to his growing American vocabulary. A brief silence followed and Bernadette's mind wandered momentarily. She thought about how relaxed she felt around Kwesi, an ease she'd come to appreciate since their journey began. She also simply missed the comfort of her grandmother and the magical stories she told. Then she remembered Kwesi's extraordinary story.

"Were you telling the truth about flowers coming out of your guitar?" Bernadette asked.

Kwesi smiled. "You don't believe it?"

"I'll believe it when I see it."

"Well, let me show you," Kwesi said, taking her hand.

He led Bernadette to his room, careful not to cause a ruckus. She was somewhat uneasy, even nervous. Although Bernadette knew her actions were harmless, being alone with Kwesi in his room felt wrong. Then she convinced herself that the closer she was to Kwesi, the less suspicious he would be of them. Bernadette sat on the edge of the bed, her eyes darting around the sparsely furnished room. Kwesi plugged his guitar cable into the amplifier and a red light illuminated. He struck a chord and slid his fingers across the frets, letting out a high-pitched sound.

Then Kwesi paused; he had never shown anyone this before. *Why now?* he thought. *Why her?* But he felt something with Bernadette he couldn't deny. Since that first trance they experienced together at his concert, he'd wanted to invite her into his world, even if for a short time. So he said, "I think you should know that you are the first person to witness this. Not even my band members have seen what my guitar can do."

Kwesi closed his eyes and played a series of arpeggios. An ethereal air swept through the room and a flurry of flowers slowly bloomed out of the amplifier. Bernadette gasped, in awe of the fantastical atmosphere. She spun around, catching the petals in her hands as they dissolved into thin air. The room had become a labyrinth of wonder and beauty. Bernadette found herself in Kwesi's arms and it wasn't for show this time, her alluring him.

Kwesi searched Bern's eyes and held them, locked his fingers within hers and pulled her close until they could feel each other's breath. She closed her eyes, an invitation to Kwesi, one he'd been hoping for. They kissed and suddenly a force lifted them in the air. They slowly levitated as a whirlwind of flowers swirled around them. Kwesi, realizing how high off the ground they were, panicked and yanked the guitar cord out of the amplifier, sending them crashing down into his bed. The flower petals slowly disappeared. Kwesi and Bernadette breathed heavily as they gazed at the wobbly ceiling fan oscillating above them. Bernadette touched her lips, turned to Kwesi, then leapt out of the bed, conscious of what had just happened. "Sorry, I have to go," she said. Kwesi, equally disoriented, nodded.

As BERNADETTE HURRIED to her room, she felt her heart pounding heavily. Melvin was snoring when she tiptoed quietly inside. She grabbed her diary and scribbled the date:

January 4th, 1966.

Bernadette was about to write the details of what had just happened with Kwesi. Then she stopped abruptly. What if Melvin somehow got his hands on her diary? He would never forgive her for her actions. So Bernadette tucked her diary in her bag and ran a bath instead. A mélange of conflicting emotions swirled inside her as she stared at her reflection in the ripples. Did she still love Melvin? Of course. They'd been so close to marriage before the night that changed everything. But if Bernadette was honest, she blamed him for their current predicament, and his anger only seemed to flare and intensify in this new environment. He spoke reassurance, but he wasn't living it.

Bernadette slid into the bathtub and was soon submerged. She cast her mind back to when she first saw Kwesi onstage.

Their instant connection and mystical bond. She had never thought about cheating on Melvin. It never crossed her mind, even though he accused her of the possibility many times. But something was changing inside her, and she concluded that it was less about her desire for Kwesi and more about her frustrations with Melvin.

CHAPTER 7

There was an indignant air on the bus the next morning, and it lasted throughout the afternoon. It could have been the stiff mattresses at the Akosombo lodge, which guaranteed that no one got a good night's sleep. Or the bout of diarrhea that wrecked T's stomach in the morning, forcing Ato to pull over twice for his excursions to the bush. Or Kwesi and Bernadette's guilty consciences about their kiss in his room. Or Melvin, beginning to sense that an affair between the two of them could be imminent.

The bottom line was that no one was in a good mood when the bus approached a roadblock swarming with festivalgoers. Ato slammed on the brakes. "They are not going to let us pass through for at least an hour." That was a conservative estimate, because everyone knew that street festivals lasted much longer than an hour. They had two options. They could take a detour and drive on the unpaved roads, or wait until the festival procession had passed. Kwesi checked his watch and did the math. "Sorry, we just have to wait." He threw his Pentax camera around his shoulder and disappeared into the crowd of women dancing in synchronized movements. T, whose stomach was still discombobulated, rushed out with pieces of newspaper in search of a public latrine. After briefly observing the festivities from the bus window, Melvin turned to Bernadette. "Let's go see what this is all about, babe." He took off his pastor's collar and grabbed his shoulder bag where he kept all his money.

Bernadette was glad to see a semblance of her old Melvin back. He waved at the children carrying little drums and joined the women dancing backward. Melvin paused to buy a newspaper and two stalks of roasted corn from an old lady wearing a large woven hat. Then a slight commotion stirred the crowd and everyone gazed at the horizon. The paramount chief was hoisted in a majestic palanquin, carried by a dozen men. Hanging over him was a gold-embroidered umbrella that twirled elegantly against the magnificent skies. The paramount chief danced with graceful hand gestures as they carried him through the crowd. Melvin and Bernadette stood in awe, mystified by the regal display of tradition, centuries old. As the crowd moved on and the streets began to open up, Melvin turned to Bernadette. "I'm sorry I've been such a jerk, babe." She smiled, pinched his nose with the tip of her finger, and replied, "You have been quite a jerk, Mel, but I forgive you. And I'm sorry if my being close to Kwesi upset you. I think having him on our side is for the best."

Melvin pulled her close and kissed her gently. She closed her eyes and remembered why she fell for him in the first place. He was not an easy man to love, she knew that. The pain of his childhood and the unresolved trauma of war had forced Melvin to grow an impenetrable shell. He was just beginning to let her in when tragedy struck on that rainy night in Alabama. Now Bernadette hoped, in their moment of reconciliation, that perhaps they could return to some normalcy when this was all over. Maybe make a home in Ghana and put the past behind them once and for all. It was the first time she'd hoped for anything beyond safety since they fled America. Kwesi came trotting back, almost out of breath. "Did you see them carrying the chief?"

"Yes, that was amazing," Bernadette replied.

"I've never seen anything like it," Melvin added, telling himself he would try to make the rest of their journey amicable.

Kwesi hung the camera around his neck. "I took some good photos of the women dancing."

"Why do they dance backward?" Melvin asked as he lit a cigarette.

"It's called Agbadza, it's supposed to be historical, something to do with their ancestors."

THE HISTORY KWESI alluded to was the genesis of the Ewe people. They lived in captivity for many years under a cruel king. He built a tall mud wall around the Ewe people and brutalized them. The tribe planned their escape by asking all the women to pour their washing water in one particular place on the mud wall.

"That was a very good plan," Kwesi said, turning his camera to Bernadette.

Eventually, the spot where the women poured water weakened. In the middle of the night, the wall collapsed and the tribe escaped. They walked backward so that their footprints couldn't be traced, and eventually they settled near the Volta Lake, where they celebrate every year.

"Fascinating," Melvin said, as he tossed his cigarette.

. . .

IT WAS LATE afternoon when the bus pulled into Jasikan. They had gone from a smooth asphalt highway to a craggy gravel road that cut through a dense thicket. The protruding branches whacked the roof of the bus and everyone jerked back and forth with every pothole they encountered. The open windows reflected the sun, and Melvin, pensive, rummaged through the newspapers. He was relieved to find that there was still no mention of him or Bernadette. As the bus continued along the bumpy road, Bernadette savored the last pages of her copy of *Jet* magazine. The story was about Black GIs stationed in Vietnam. On the last page of the magazine was an advertisement for the new Volkswagen Beetle.

In bold black letters it read: *BE A MODERN MAN, DRIVE A BUGGY.*

The image of a debonair gentleman standing next to a black Volkswagen reminded Bernadette of Alabama, and the night they fled Otto's Diner.

THE WIND GUSTS and rain pelted Bernadette as they drove toward 85 North. She buried her head under Melvin's coat, trembling with pieces of broken glass under her feet. Melvin wiped his eyes with the back of his hand to clear his blurry vision flooded with rain, sweat, and fear. They had driven in silence for what felt like forever. Then, Melvin suddenly veered off the interstate and pulled over. Bernadette flung off the wet coat that was her only shelter. "What you doing, Mel?"

Melvin cut the headlights and darkness engulfed them. The crescent moon illuminated the sleek silver trimmings of the Chevrolet Impala. Melvin whispered to Bernadette in a low tone, "Hand me the book, babe." Bernadette popped the glove compartment open and passed Melvin the *Green Book*. He flipped through it and murmured almost to himself, "There's a Negro-owned garage fifteen minutes ahead, Odell's Auto Service."

Suddenly, an eerie rustling sound echoed through the woods, startling them. Melvin quickly turned the key in the ignition and it squealed, signaling an engine already running. He flicked on the headlights and a shadowy figure dashed across the road. "You see that?" Melvin asked, hoping it was a figment of his imagination.

Bernadette nodded slowly. "Let's get outta here, Mel."

Melvin slammed on the gas, and wet gravel splattered under the screeching tires.

THE STREETS OF LaGrange, Georgia, were deserted when they pulled into town. Nobody saw the Impala with a busted windshield floating by stealthily. Melvin's eyes searched for Odell's Auto Service. "The book said it should be right here on Greenville Street," Melvin whispered, eyes peeled and alert.

"There it is," Bernadette said, pointing at a decrepit building with a hand-painted sign loosely hanging from the gate.

The letter O had peeled off, so it just said *dell's Auto*.

An old man wearing baggy blue overalls was locking the gate when the headlights illuminated the building. He raised his hand against the light and Melvin cut the engine off. The old man limped cautiously toward the car, pausing to observe the busted windshield and the pair of petrified eyes staring back at him. He gnawed on a cigar that lit half of his face through the billowing smoke he exhaled. "Y'all had some trouble, I see," he said in a low, croaky tone.

Melvin nodded.

"Well, I was just about done here, but I can open up for a li'l bit."

He lifted up the large aluminum gate and motioned them inside.

"I'm Odell by the way, most people call me Dell, on account of my sign."

THE INTERIOR OF the garage was just as wretched as the exterior. A pair of fluorescent tubes brightened the dusty tarps that covered the carcasses of broken automobiles. Odell opened the mini fridge and grabbed two cans of Pepsi-Cola. Then he pulled out folding chairs for Melvin and Bernadette. "So," he said, blowing a thick circle of smoke, "I ain't gonna ask y'all what happened, but I reckon ya need a new windshield, right?"

Melvin nodded, subdued and torpid.

"Well, that ain't gonna happen till next Tuesday, and that's being mighty optimistic." Bernadette took a gulp of the Pepsi-Cola, still shivering under the wet coat. Her mind drifted momentarily. Could Melvin really get them out of this? Would they be better off surrendering to the police?

Odell extinguished the last chunk of his cigar in a glass ashtray. "It ain't easy getting parts for this here Chevrolet, certainly not around here."

Melvin buried his face in his palm. A headache was splitting his skull apart. He felt the poke of the Colt .45 pistol in his pocket and remembered he had to discard it soon. Odell leaned forward, arching his eyebrows. "Where y'all heading, if you don't mind me asking?"

"Philadelphia," Melvin said.

"When y'all 'spose to be there?"

"By morning."

Odell limped to his desk, ruminating on an idea.

"Now, y'all know that ain't gonna happen. But if you absolutely, positively, need to be in Philadelphia tomorrow, I can trade y'all for that Chevrolet."

Melvin shot Bernadette a glance as Odell flipped a tarp covering one of the cars. It sent a thick cloud of dust into the air. Their faces dropped with disappointment when the dust settled and they saw a raggedy black Volkswagen Beetle. "It don't look like much, but it's dependable as a rock," Odell said, trying to sell it. Melvin inspected the Volkswagen thoroughly. When he was satisfied, he exchanged keys with Odell.

THE VOLKSWAGEN HAD a quirky steering wheel that made for a nervous drive. Melvin adjusted his seat to accommodate the narrow gear box, and after seven uncomfortable hours, it was clear that trading a brand-new Impala for an old, decaying Volkswagen was truly moronic. He consoled himself knowing that in a few hours, police in every state would be looking for a black Chevrolet with a broken windshield. So, with all its discomforts, the Volkswagen was their saving grace.

Bernadette was still asleep when the early vestiges of sunrise beamed across the horizon. Melvin lit a cigarette as he pulled over on the Roanoke River Bridge. He could see the vast Virginian plains and it made him nostalgic. The early-morning dew had fogged the car windows, refracting beams from the streetlights that lit the empty bridge. Melvin glanced at Bernadette sleeping peacefully, and a deep cathartic feeling descended on him. He had really fucked up this time, he thought. Melvin dug out the Colt .45 pistol from his pocket, opened the car door quietly, and strolled to the railing of the bridge. He flung the pistol into the lake, and an ominous splash reverberated below. The sound woke Bernadette, and she saw Melvin sobbing on the bridge. She had never seen him in such a helpless state. Bernadette thought about stepping out and consoling him, but she decided against it. Her sympathy would only embarrass him. So Bernadette pretended to be fast asleep when Melvin finally wiped the tears from his eyes and stepped back into the old tottering Volkswagen.

CHAPTER 8

It had been two whole days of driving when the bus finally pulled up to Dambai. It was the only ferry point for vehicles traveling across the Volta Lake. The lush vegetation made for a gnarly ride through the village. The band had traveled on this road before, en route to the Upper Volta. Subsequently, Ato anticipated the malignant wild boars that roamed the grove.

"Holy shit, what the fuck was that?" Melvin yelled, pointing at the passel of boars speeding through the bush.

Everyone burst out laughing except Ato. "For a pastor, you use a lot of bad language, sah," Ato said, glancing disapprovingly at Melvin through the rearview mirror. Ato was one of those newly baptized Christians who took blasphemy seriously. Bernadette also pinched Melvin's hand discreetly, a subtle reminder that they had an act to keep up.

THE BUS PULLED up to a ferry boat docked on the lake. A young man with a solid physique stepped aboard the flat deck. He motioned forward and Ato eased the bus atop the ferry. A slight swaying sensation rocked the bus as they set sail across the tranquil Volta Lake.

All the passengers passed out except Melvin. He had grown anxious about reuniting with Nkrumah, so he stepped off the bus to clear his head. Out of habit, Melvin grabbed his shoulder bag full of cash. He leaned against the ferry rail and observed the superfluous vegetation that flanked the lake. Melvin felt the urge to urinate, and without thinking, he hung his shoulder bag on the edge of the rail. As he peed, a gust of air throttled the ferry. Melvin's bag slid into the lake with a soft splash. He panicked, attempted to jump into the water, but remembered he couldn't swim. The young man who worked on the ferry dove into the frigid lake and retrieved the bag. He swam to the deck and handed it to Melvin, who was still paralyzed with shock. Melvin unzipped the bag and was relieved to find that the insulated lining had protected the cash from water damage. He thanked the young man with a tip and drained the remaining water from the bag. When Melvin was alone, he thumbed through the banknotes, his entire life savings, which was supposed to be his down payment for the car dealership. The money was still wrapped in the currency strips from United Bank, where he had made a withdrawal on the day they fled Philadelphia.

IT HAD TAKEN the Volkswagen thirteen hours to get from Odell's Auto Service to South Philly. Besides an incident in Richmond where a police patrol car followed them for thirty miles, the drive was relatively uneventful. True to Odell's word, the Volkswagen wasn't much to look at, but it was dependable. Bernadette had been scanning the radio for news somewhere around Maryland, when she heard the words "Otto's Diner."

Melvin pulled over and they listened to the entire broadcast. It vaguely described a Negro couple driving a black Chevrolet Impala. The Alabama police chief urged the public to be vigilant, and to consider the fugitives "armed and dangerous."

"What we gonna do, Mel?" Bernadette whispered.

Melvin glanced at her, eyes bloodshot and fatigued. "We could turn ourselves in, but that ain't gonna end well, Bern. I killed a white man in Alabama, that's the electric chair. They gon' say you my accomplice. Ain't no way around that."

They sat in silence, watching the green trolley totter down the street.

"We gotta run, babe," Melvin finally said.

"Run? Where we gonna run to, Mel?"

"Africa."

"Africa?"

"Yes, Bern, Africa. I got a friend there, he's the president of Ghana now. He gon' take care of us, I guarantee it."

"What you talking about, Mel?"

Melvin went on to tell Bernadette about that fateful night on the Lincoln University train tracks. He shared the details of how he'd saved his friend's life and reiterated the promise Nkrumah had made. Bernadette remained hesitant, however. How could they be sure that President Nkrumah would harbor them? Besides, Melvin had committed the murder, not her. Why should she sacrifice her freedom for him?

But Melvin remained unequivocal that they were accomplices.

"No one's gonna believe you, babe. We either flee or face the chair together."

Bernadette searched her mind for an alternative but found none. After brooding for a while, Melvin laid out the scenario for their escape.

Their journey to Ghana required passports, which they had fortunately acquired in anticipation of their honeymoon. They would also need cash. Melvin intended to withdraw his entire life savings from the United Bank of Philadelphia. Lastly, they would need a place to lay low. The only person Melvin trusted was his old army buddy Corey.

COREY LAMONT JONES had served in the 761st Tank Battalion with Melvin. They met in Würzburg before their unit was deployed to Vic-sur-Seille, a strategic restocking point for the Nazis. Their mission was to capture the town and set up a blockade. Under the cover of darkness, Melvin read out the coordinates for a strike, and Corey loaded the shells into the main gun. "Fire on command," a voice resounded through their headsets. Melvin locked the tank scope and aimed it at a church steeple where German snipers had been hiding. He fired the shell and the steeple exploded, obliterating it. The panicked voice of the commander yelled, "Twelve o'clock! Twelve o'clock!" Melvin peeked through the hatch doors and saw a German tanker aimed directly at them. Before he could turn the turret, a shell blasted through their hatch, exploding the tank. Their commander and driver were killed instantly. Melvin helped Corey, who was bleeding from a shrapnel cut. The two men crept underneath the tank and waited.

Soon, two Nazi officers rushed out to inspect the smoldering tank. Melvin, sensing this was their only chance, remembered what he had learned in basic training. The art of disarming an enemy combatant. He leapt up from behind, twisted the officer's hand, and shot him with his own gun. Corey jumped up and slashed the remaining Nazi officer with his knife. They recovered their rifles and ran into a building across the street. A sound rattled from the kitchen and Melvin kicked in the door to see a wide-eyed woman and her two small children.

"Nous sommes français! Nous sommes français!" the woman yelled as she raised her hands. Melvin lowered the gun and turned to see Corey, limping with his bloody leg. The woman dug out a first-aid kit from the kitchen cabinet and Melvin dressed Corey's wound. As they hid in the dark kitchen, Corey whispered, "What we gon' do if them Krauts find us here, Mel?" Melvin cocked the rifle, handed it to Corey, and said, "You gonna need this. Ain't no brother of mine gonna be taken alive."

Suddenly, a flurry of bombs exploded, shattering the kitchen windows. Melvin was relieved to hear the word "Flash," to which he responded "Thunder," a code the U.S. Army used to identify each other. The 101st Airborne Division surrounded Vic-sur-Seille, and the few remaining Nazi officers surrendered. Melvin stayed with Corey until he was airlifted to a hospital that night.

It took a whole year after the war for Melvin and Corey to reunite. They both found themselves in the lobby of the veterans center, waiting for their psychiatric counseling appointments. Needless to say, it was an emotional reconnection. So, as Melvin pondered who he could trust to harbor them temporarily, Corey was the only person who came to mind. Before heading to Corey's, however, Melvin and Bernadette stopped at their apartment in Germantown. They hurriedly packed their clothes and passports. Bernadette grabbed her leather-bound diary, Ma' Susan's note, and her mermaid totem. Melvin took his Phi Beta Sigma photograph with Kwame Nkrumah. Then he lit a smoldering fire in the sink, burning all remaining documents.

COREY LIVED ON a sketchy corner of 11th and Morris streets, across from a hardware store. The sanitation workers' strike had left mountains of garbage piled on every street corner. It reeked of death and decay, attracting vermin of all sizes and shapes. Melvin had to park the Volkswagen a whole block ahead, just so Bernadette could alight without trudging through the pungent heap.

The buzzer rattled. "Who that is?"

Melvin leaned forward. "It's me, Melvin."

"Melvin who?" the voice stuttered back.

"Army Mel, open up."

A buzzing sound echoed and Melvin led Bernadette through a dilapidated foyer toward a spiral staircase. Corey was standing at his door with his arms folded and a loose cigarette hanging out of his thick mustache. He ushered them inside quietly and locked the door.

"Shit, soon as I heard a nigga driving a Chevy done shot a white man, I prayed to God it wasn't you," Corey said, lighting his cigarette. "It's on the radio every hour, Mel."

Bernadette's anxious eyes scanned the ramshackle apartment. A photograph of Corey in his army uniform hung on the wall. A brown corduroy couch sat across from a small black-and-white television.

"This is Bernadette, my fiancée," Melvin said, easing into the couch.

Corey limped over to Bernadette and shook her hand. "Nice to make your acquaintance, ma'am. Heard a lot about you." Corey grabbed a chair, flipped it around, and asked, "So what the plan is?" The plan, according to Melvin, was to lay low for a couple hours, withdraw his life savings from the bank, purchase one-way tickets to Ghana, and never look back.

WHAT MELVIN DIDN'T know, however, was that a tenacious FBI agent had already tracked down the Chevrolet Impala and was currently dusting for fingerprints in Odell's shop. Agent Hughes was a clean-shaven white man with slicked-back hair parted on one side. He had a dedicated air about him, deliberate and singularly focused. His jaws ground mechanically when he interrogated suspects, and it made Odell nervous.

"Hell, I ain't know who they was. They just came up in here with them big ol' guns, talking 'bout, we taking this here Volkswagen, make a move and we'll shoot you."

"And why didn't you call the police after they left?" Agent Hughes asked, scribbling in his notepad.

"Shit, I was scared. They said they gonna come back and kill me. Would you call the police if it was you?"

Agent Hughes wrote down the missing VW's license plate and left the local LaGrange Sheriff's Department to finish taking Odell's statement. Then he drove toward 85 North in the Lincoln Continental he'd rented in Washington, D.C. Cruising down the empty highway, Agent Hughes felt a sharp pain in his chest. He dug in his breast pocket, flipped the cover off his medication, swallowed a pill, and washed it down with a can of root beer. The palpitations subsided, and he was grateful that they weren't as severe as they were six months ago when they first started.

IT WAS MID-JULY and Agent Hughes had just been assigned to the Fort Lauderdale jet pack robbery, a bizarre conundrum that plagued the Federal Bureau of Investigation. Agent Hughes reviewed the facts on his first day:

> *At approximately 2 pm on July 7th 1965, a man identi-*
> *fied as John Petty walked into the parking lot of the Fort*
> *Lauderdale First National Bank. A Brink's armored truck*
> *was delivering an estimated $400,000 to the bank. Mr.*
> *Petty electrocuted both security guards with a cattle prod,*
> *took two bags of cash, and disappeared into a nearby*
> *thicket. Then a mechanical sound shook the trees, and*
> *Mr. Petty shot up in the sky, wearing a jet pack and carry-*
> *ing the bags of cash. He is suspected to have landed*
> *somewhere in the Everglades, but no conclusive evidence*
> *confirmed it.*

Agent Hughes and the local Fort Lauderdale Sheriff's Department combed the Everglades for traces of hydrogen peroxide, a substance John Petty used to power his propulsion rocket.

As the search went from days to weeks, it caused a media circus that raised a number of questions. Did John Petty survive the jet pack flight? If so, how did he travel through the Everglades? Were there other accomplices?

That was when an anonymous tip divulged that a man

matching John Petty's description paid cash for a boat in Miami and sailed to Cuba. The Bureau was against Agent Hughes expanding his investigation to a foreign territory. But after persisting for a week, he convinced his superiors that a successful apprehension was imminent and got the green light to travel to Cuba.

When Agent Hughes arrived in Havana, his CIA liaison informed him that the Cuban authorities were holding the man suspected to be John Petty. Through back-door channels, Agent Hughes was granted access to the man and he immediately realized that the suspect wasn't John Petty. He was just an ordinary gringo who had stolen his wife's inheritance and fled to Cuba. That was when Agent Hughes first felt the heart palpitations. He lost his balance and collapsed in the Cuban jail. When he woke up, he was back in Washington with a respirator beeping in his hospital room. His failure to apprehend John Petty led to the FBI closing the case, and after six months of dormancy, Agent Hughes was finally assigned a case, Melvin and Bernadette's. So, as he drove up to Philadelphia, he planned to make up for the Cuban debacle at all costs.

BERNADETTE WAITED RESTLESSLY for Melvin at Corey's apartment. He was on his way to the Snyder Avenue Costume Shop. The rumbling sounds of Corey snoring irritated Bernadette. She glanced to see his lean frame enveloped by the large corduroy couch he had salvaged from a local shelter. It smelled like a wet stray dog and soon made Bernadette queasy. She hurried to the bathroom and thought about throwing up in the sink but changed her mind at the last minute, aiming for the toilet instead. Bernadette flushed with trembling hands. She desperately needed to tell someone about her predicament. Ella was the only person she trusted, the only one who would understand. Bernadette checked her watch. It was a quarter past four P.M. She decided she could see Ella before Melvin returned from the costume shop.

Bernadette grabbed her purse and tiptoed past Corey sleeping on the couch. She kept her head down as she shuffled briskly toward Morris Street. A group of boys brushed past her as they ran toward an ice cream truck that was parked at the intersection. That was where Bernadette saw the police squad car speeding toward her. Her heart sank. She thought about making a run for it, but her legs wouldn't move. Then the squad car made a sharp U-turn and kept driving. Bernadette exhaled deeply, temporarily relieved. She climbed aboard the trolley that was heading toward Snyder Avenue. Ten minutes later, Bernadette was once again standing in front of the burgundy two-story row house, staring at the numbers *2335* neatly arranged on the building.

ELLA CRACKED THE door open and froze. Her large eyes scanned Bernadette with intense curiosity. Then she smiled. "Girl, you pregnant, ain't you?"

"What?" Bernadette replied, a jolt of shock paralyzing her.

"I said you pregnant, ain't you? I can see it all over your—"

Bernadette's legs were the first to give out, and then her eyes rolled backward. Before she knew it, her body crashed onto the hardwood floor.

. . .

WHEN BERNADETTE REGAINED consciousness, she felt a high-pitched ringing sound in her ear. Her eyes slowly adjusted to the light and she saw Ella and Kareem framed by the door, pacing nervously.

"What happened?" Bernadette mumbled.

"May Allah be praised," Ella shouted, as she rushed toward Bernadette, who was propped feebly on the couch. Kareem closed his Qur'an and poured Bernadette a glass of water.

"How are you feeling?" he asked.

"I'm fine," Bernadette replied. "I just can't remember what happened."

Ella glanced at Kareem, and he shook his head disapprovingly.

"I think you're pregnant, Bern," Ella whispered.

"You sure?" Bernadette said in a quavering voice.

"Some things a woman just know."

Bernadette sighed. She had forgotten that her period was late, and all that throwing up had to be morning sickness. Then she remembered why she was at Ella's house in the first place. "Shit, what time is it?"

"Why? You got somewhere to be?" Ella asked exasperatedly.

"We can drive you to the hospital, if you—" Kareem started to say, but Bernadette cut him off.

"Sorry, I gotta go now."

"Have you lost your mind?" Ella screamed in disbelief. "You need to rest."

But Bernadette was already halfway out the door. Then she ran back and hugged Ella. "You were always good to me. I'll never forget that."

Then she rushed out of the house and disappeared into the evening mist.

WHEN BERNADETTE RETURNED to Corey's apartment, she leaned against the door and listened for any sign of Melvin. All she heard was Corey's obnoxious snoring, so she cracked the door gently open. Bernadette walked into the bathroom and caught her reflection in the mirror. She had become a shell of herself. Her eyes, which were once radiant, had lost their light. She thought about the family she always longed for, a soft place to land, just like her friend Ella. But Bernadette knew Melvin's apprehension about being a father. "Why spoil this good thing we have with kids," he would say whenever she brought up the subject. So Bernadette decided to keep her pregnancy a secret from Melvin. At least until she could confirm that she was indeed pregnant. She reached for her diary and wrote the date:

December 27th, 1965

Could it be? God, not now. Why now?
Me? Pregnant?
Ella seems so sure yet I can't tell Mel,
my fiancé, the father of my child.
It's all too much.

MELVIN SPENT PART of the afternoon at the costume shop. After trying on a few different clerical garments, he settled on the all-black regalia with a white pastor's collar. Satisfied with his choice, Melvin walked to the United Bank downtown, avoiding the trolleys and buses. He approached the middle-aged white lady behind the teller window and slid his withdrawal slip over the counter. The amount—fifteen thousand, two hundred and twenty dollars—was Melvin's entire life savings. The bank teller glanced suspiciously at him as she handed over the bundles of cash.

"You're sure you don't need an extra bag for that, sir?" the teller asked, watching Melvin stuff the money into his shoulder bag.

"No, ma'am," Melvin said, eager to exit the bank before she alerted anyone. Melvin's instincts were right, because shortly after he walked out, the teller called the Philadelphia police and they descended swiftly on the bank.

WHEN MELVIN FINALLY returned to Corey's apartment, Bernadette rushed to him and hugged him tightly.

"She been worried sick, bruh," Corey said. "I told her if anyone can pull this off, it's Mel. He saved me from them crazy Nazis. But she ain't believe me."

That night, Corey drove Melvin and Bernadette to the airport, taking the back roads to avoid any potential checkpoints. Melvin held it together until they drove past the empty lot in Germantown. This was all he had toiled for. His American dream. Now he had to erase it from his mind, another dream deferred. Like his father and his grandfather before him.

When Corey pulled up to the airport, he handed Melvin a .38-caliber Ruger and repeated the words Melvin had told him in Vic-sur-Seille: "You gonna need this. Ain't no brother of mine gonna be taken alive." Melvin nodded and stashed the pistol in his shoulder bag. He grabbed his Bible and led Bernadette through the sliding airport doors.

IT HAD BEEN three hours since Agent Hughes began rummaging through Melvin and Bernadette's apartment in Germantown. He stripped the furniture and combed through the ashes clogged in the sink for any clues as to where Melvin and Bernadette might be hiding. After exhausting all options, Agent Hughes slumped onto their mattress, and as a last-ditch effort, he decided to check underneath the bed. He stuck his hand deep into the dark crevice, swinging wildly until he touched a small cosmetics box. Agent Hughes pulled it out, flipped it open, and grabbed the stack of letters neatly bound with a thread. They all belonged to Bernadette, and Agent Hughes scribbled down the sender's name and address:

Ella Maxine Turner.
2335 Snyder Avenue, Philadelphia.

A SLIGHT DRIZZLE splattered against Agent Hughes's windshield as he sped down the wet road. Behind him were two police squad cars, and their bright rotating siren lights refracted through the rain as they pulled up to Ella and Kareem's doorstep.

The baby wailing in the background added to the commotion. Kareem paced back and forth mumbling Qur'an verses to himself, as Ella sat in disbelief.

"Wait—wait, Bernadette did what?"

"Yes, ma'am. She and Melvin are wanted suspects in a

murder. Tell me how you knew she was pregnant," Agent Hughes asked as he scribbled in his notepad.

"I just knew."

"Are there visible signs? Is she showing?"

"No—but I knew."

"How long was she here?"

"It was an hour, tops. She passed out as soon as she got here. She ain't mention nothing about no killings neither."

"Okay. And for the last time, you don't know where she went?"

"No, sir. She didn't say."

Kareem glanced at the police officers combing through the living room.

"Do we have to get a lawyer?" he asked, handing the baby to Ella.

"Not if you are telling the truth," Agent Hughes replied.

Then an officer rushed in. "Sir, we just apprehended a known associate of the suspects, he was returning from the airport." The officer checked his notes. "His name is Corey Jones, sir."

Agent Hughes tucked his notepad in his breast pocket. He slid his card onto the table, eyes fixed on Ella and Kareem. "Call me as soon as you hear from her."

THE BLARING POLICE sirens startled the crowd of passengers at the airport departure terminal. Agent Hughes pulled over and dashed out, neglecting to shut the car door. He sprinted past the security gates, flashing his FBI badge at the equally frightened customs officers. When he finally arrived at the boarding gate, Agent Hughes was out of breath, and his chest palpitations began to flare. A group of uniformed police officers walked toward him with dejected faces, and his heart sank. They had missed the flight by a mere ten minutes. Agent Hughes slammed the ticket counter, flustered and raging. How could he let Melvin and Bernadette get away? He loosened his tie and sank into one of the lobby seats, gazing out the airport window at the kaleidoscope of flights arriving and departing. At that moment, he concocted a plan that would have far-reaching consequences. Two days later, without telling his FBI superiors, Agent Hughes purchased a one-way ticket to Ghana.

CHAPTER 9

The ferry took about half an hour to cross the Volta Lake. All the passengers in the bus were wiping remnants of sleep from their eyes when they docked. Bernadette slowly ran her hand over her womb, grateful for yet another safe journey. Melvin was still dozing when the ferry anchored. "He's a deep sleeper," Bernadette said, glancing at Kwesi. He avoided Bernadette's eyes. "About last night, in my room, I'm—" Bernadette raised her finger to her lips, and Kwesi stopped short.

THE VILLAGE THAT sat beyond the lake was something out of a postcard. The forest trees and picturesque mountains made for an excellent rest stop. The village was also home to the largest group of wild peacocks, and they spread their elaborately colored feathers as Ato parked the bus under a tall verdant tree. The villagers, mostly clad in wax prints, walked toward the only brick building that stood among a cluster of thatched-roof huts, each holding a Bible. A short, bearded man dressed in a priestly robe approached the bus window.

"Are you joining our revival?" he asked.

Ato, without taking a survey of his passengers, blurted, "Yes, Pastor."

Kwesi and T protested quietly, but Ato assured them that the revival should only last an hour. "But how do you know this?" Kwesi asked, baffled.

"God told me," Ato said, without a hint of sarcasm.

"God told you?" Kwesi asked, now seething.

"Yes, Kwesi. I talk to God all the time and he tells me things."

Kwesi shook his head and reluctantly joined the group heading to the church.

THE WHITE STONE walls of the Redeemed Anglican Church absorbed the beams of light pouring through the stained-glass windows. Melvin sat uncomfortably in a pew next to Bernadette. His pastor's collar was soaked from the impregnable humidity that hung menacingly over the congregation. Kwesi, T, and the twins were seething with anger, upset that Ato had roped them into his newly baptized Christian fervor. Behind the ornate pulpit was a portrait of the whitest Jesus that Bernadette had ever seen. His crown of thorns sat on his long blond hair. A bright halo glowed above him, and he raised his fingers, as if pledging the scout's honor. Bernadette shook her head and sighed. "Even in Africa, white Jesus is everywhere."

It had been this way since the early missionaries arrived in the Gold Coast, one of whom was Anglican bishop Joseph Clarke. Together with the villagers, Bishop Clarke built the brick church, a first of its kind in West Africa. However, he underestimated the humidity, because a month after the church was completed, he collapsed and died of heatstroke in the middle of a sermon. His trusted translator, Fofo Kwadzo, had assumed the pastor's duties until the archbishop in Scotland found a suitable replacement.

"Our lord and master Jesus has brought us some visitors today," Fofo Kwadzo said, gesturing at Melvin, Bernadette, Kwesi, and the band. "Can you tell us where you are from?"

Ato nudged Melvin with his elbow, and he stood reluctantly. "I'm Pastor Johnson from America," Melvin said groggily, eyes moving through the curious faces in the congregation. "This is my wife, and these are my flock."

The translator rambled in Ewe. When he finished, a loud applause rang out in the church. Melvin sat down slowly, admitting to himself that he would have to do better if he was ever called upon again.

Soon the church was pulsating with fervent praise and worship music. The collection basket made its way around the congregation, and Bernadette realized that the worshippers were a fanatic bunch. Some danced between the pews; others, imbued with the Holy Ghost, murmured in tongues. After Fofo Kwadzo's ardent sermon came the odd spectacle of deliverance. It was unlike anything Melvin and Bernadette had ever seen. Fofo Kwadzo pressed his hands on the forehead of each parishioner, until they were delivered by the Holy Spirit. This act usually culminated with the parishioner collapsing on the floor or pew. Kwesi, T, Ato, and the twins quickly went down when Fofo Kwadzo touched their foreheads. Bernadette took the cue, jerked back and forth, and pretended to collapse too. Melvin, however, was defiant. He disliked the charade and refused to fall down. The longer he resisted, the harder Fofo Kwadzo pressed on his forehead.

"Evil spirit, I command you to leave the pastor alone."

"Amen," the congregation shouted.

"Arababababakalashahada. In the name of Jesus, I command you, evil spirit, release the pastor now."

"Amen." The congregation got louder.

"Holy Spirit, take control of the pastor."

Bernadette, realizing Melvin was being stubborn, kicked his leg from under the pew. Melvin winced from the sharp pain and turned to see Bernadette prostrated on the floor, mouthing the words *Just fall down.*

Melvin ignored her, and she kicked him again, harder.

"Just fall down, Mel," she muttered.

Melvin finally gave up and dropped to the ground amid cheers from the congregation.

"Hallelujah—Amen," they shouted as Fofo Kwadzo waved his moist handkerchief in the air. "The devil will never win in the house of God," he shouted.

WHEN THE REVIVAL was over, Melvin was livid. "That's just a sham," he whispered to Bernadette. "That man ain't got no healing powers."

"It don't even matter, Mel. You're supposed to be a pastor, act like one so we can get the hell outta here."

The parishioners exchanged handshakes and hugs, reserving extra vivacity for their American guests. Fofo Kwadzo tried to convince Melvin to stay for dinner, but he wasn't having it. As the bus sped away from the church, Kwesi heard the radio forecast predicting a tropical storm, and it made him apprehensive.

❈

THE ACCRA AIRPORT was larger than Agent Hughes imagined. The arrivals hall was separated into two categories. One area for Ghanaian citizens, and the other for foreigners. Under normal circumstances, a representative from the U.S. State Department would have met Agent Hughes on the tarmac and walked him through a special processing facility. But these weren't normal circumstances. His superiors didn't even know he was in Ghana yet. So when the Ghanaian customs officer arched his eyebrow and asked, "Business or pleasure?" Agent Hughes responded emphatically, "Pleasure."

Just as he expected, the Ghanaian humidity was vicious. He unfurled his suit jacket, loosened his tie, and glanced across the street at an aqua-blue Peugeot. The man behind the wheel was Frank Dekker, a veteran CIA field agent. He came highly recommended by Agent Hughes's colleague in the Bureau.

"Oh man, I gotta tell ya, he's responsible for more overthrows in the third world than any other CIA agent I know," Agent Graham said right before he kicked the vending machine that refused to deliver his can of soda. "Don't tell him I gave you his contact, though, he likes to stay low-key, if you know what I mean."

As Agent Hughes gazed at Frank Dekker, there was nothing low-key about him. If his long blond hair, Ray-Ban shades, and finger rings weren't flamboyant enough, surely his colorful Hawaiian shirt and bell-bottom pants made him stick out like a sore thumb in the streets of Accra.

"You must be Hughes," Frank Dekker said with a New York accent, South Bronx to be exact.

"You must be Frank," Agent Hughes said, shaking Frank Dekker's hand firmly.

Agent Hughes stuffed his suitcase in the trunk of the Peugeot, and Frank Dekker started the engine. They drove down the busy airport street and took the roundabout toward central Accra.

The midafternoon sun reflected off Frank Dekker's sunglasses, obscuring a scar across his right eye—a souvenir from the overthrow of Mohammad Mosaddegh in Iran. That was Frank Dekker's first mission, if you didn't count his brief stint in Bolivia, where he helped establish a military junta against President Víctor Paz Estenssoro.

Notwithstanding his current status, Frank Dekker's journey to the CIA was less than savory. He was born in the South Bronx to Dutch immigrant parents. His father abandoned him at birth and his mother helped put him through Fordham University. That was where he was recruited by the CIA. He worked at the Washington office as a field agent and was sent to Bolivia to foment a coup against then president Estenssoro. After a successful mission in Bolivia, Frank Dekker took a special interest in Africa, destabilizing newly independent governments and installing despots loyal to the West. Whether it was Egypt, the Congo, Rhodesia, or Ghana, his mission was always the same—protect American interests and thwart Russian influence.

"I hear you're on a quick in-and-out mission," Frank Dekker said, flipping the cover off his chrome lighter. He ignited a neatly rolled joint and Agent Hughes could now see the details of Frank Dekker's rings, all skulls and bones.

"Yes," Agent Hughes replied.

"Well, we got some company business here, real high-level, so I suggest you do what you gotta do real quick and skedaddle."

Agent Hughes nodded. *Company* was code for the CIA, and Agent Hughes assumed they had something big planned, but he knew better than to ask what.

"Agent Graham gave you my contact, right?" Frank Dekker asked, drawing a toke of his joint. Agent Hughes responded with a sullen shrug.

"Damn, I knew it. That son of a bitch always does this shit. You at least get clearance from the Bureau to be here?"

"Of course," Agent Hughes said, averting his eyes.

A DARK CLUSTER of rain clouds blotted out the sky. The bus meandered slowly and Ato often pumped the brakes to avoid swerving off into the deep ditches on either side of the road. They drove by a eucalyptus farm, and the fragrance lingered in the bus. Bernadette inhaled the familiar minty scent and it reminded her of Ma' Susan. She flipped open her diary and pulled out Ma' Susan's note:

My Water Baby.
You have a purpose.
Find it.
Love, Grand Ma.

Bernadette placed the note over her stomach and smiled. Maybe that was her purpose, she thought. Then Bernadette glanced at Melvin, sleeping peacefully in his seat. She would tell him about the baby when she was ready. Perhaps after they met President Nkrumah and Melvin was back in a good mood. A rain droplet splattered the window, interrupting Bernadette's musings. Then a flurry of droplets rattled the roof, followed by a thunderstorm that pummeled the bus, forcing Ato to pull over.

CHAPTER 10

The Ambassador Hotel was the recommended lodging for expats in Ghana. A bright chandelier illuminated the large foyer, which was crowded with guests at the reception desk. A variety of languages and dialects floated through the lobby as Agent Hughes checked in and waited for the elevator. His room was on the fourth floor, facing the Accra industrial area. When he parted the curtains, he saw the chaotic streets filled with buses, rickshaws, and trucks. Clouds of exhaust fumes swallowed the vehicles zooming in and out of warehouses. The hotel room had a stale smell. A mixture of humidity, cigarettes, and sex, hard-baked into the thin walls. Agent Hughes dug out Melvin's and Bernadette's photographs and dialed a number on the rotary phone. It was four P.M. in Accra, which made it eleven A.M. in Washington. He guessed the Bureau's morning briefing would be over by now.

"Hello, Hughes? Fitzgerald is fuckin' pissed, man. He said you weren't authorized to leave?"

Agent Hughes lodged the phone between his shoulder and his cheek, pinning the photos of Melvin and Bernadette on the wall. "Connect me to Fitzgerald's desk, please."

✳

TORRENTIAL RAIN PUMMELED the bus for two whole hours with no respite. A flash of lightning occasionally illuminated the dense clouds, ushering a rumbling, thunderous clap. Ato had parked the bus on the side of the road after attempts to drive through the pelting rain proved futile. Kwesi checked his watch one more time. "It could rain for two days nonstop in this area."

"How many more hours do we have to drive?" Bernadette asked, knowing Melvin was thinking the same.

"Ten hours at least," Kwesi replied. But that didn't take into account the delays due to flooding, collapsed bridges, and rest stops. In reality, it was more like fifteen hours, which meant they would miss Nkrumah's gala altogether. Ato, feeling somewhat responsible for losing time at the church, offered up a solution.

"We can take the train, look," he said, tracing his hand along the map. "It is about thirty minutes walking to the Wulensi station. Then we can catch the train to Bawku, which is only a twenty-minute drive to Kulungugu."

Kwesi's eyes lit up, scrutinizing the map.

Then T blurted, "This is a stupid idea. I'm not walking in this." He pointed beyond the window as a harsh wind tore a few limbs from a tree.

Kwesi turned to the twins, and they too shook their heads defiantly. This was a quagmire for him. He could forfeit the show, but that would mean passing up the opportunity to join President Nkrumah's official band on their North America trip. Kwesi couldn't bear the thought of it, so he decided he would venture out alone and give a solo performance.

"I will come with you, sah," Ato said.

"No," Kwesi shot back. "Wait for the rain to stop, drive back, and find me some new musicians." Kwesi turned to Melvin and Bernadette. "I'm sorry you did not get to see all of the real Ghana, maybe next time."

"We can come with you," Bernadette said, trying to sound nonchalant.

"Really?" Kwesi replied excitedly. Then he glanced at Melvin.

"Hey, we've come this far." Melvin shrugged.

THE *DAILY GRAPHIC* office sat on the second floor of a large warehouse in Accra. The rotating industrial fan did little to curb the heat. Even with a storm pounding the corrugated roof, the humidity was suffocating. The constant grinding of the newspaper printing machine aggravated Agent Hughes. He dabbed the sweat from his flushed red face.

"The reward is one thousand cedis if it leads to their arrest," he yelled, competing with the grinding mechanical noise. A flabby gentleman sat across from him snoring loudly. He had fallen asleep midsentence for the third time, and Agent Hughes concluded that he must be narcoleptic. What shitty luck. Of all the journalists in this noisy newspaper office he had to choose the narcoleptic. After waiting a few minutes Agent Hughes gently nudged the man's arm and he jerked forward, wiping the drool that had leaked onto his cheek with the back of his hand.

"I'm sorry, sah. Did I fall asleep again?"

"Yes, you did. The reward is one thousand cedis if it leads

to their arrest," he shouted, fearing the man might fall asleep again.

To his surprise, the man picked up Melvin's and Bernadette's photographs, scrutinizing them intensely. Then he pushed back his chair and lodged his glasses in his thick hair. "Okay, I cannot promise that we can publish this evening, but I will check with my editors."

Agent Hughes sighed deeply. "Anything you can do to expedite this will be appreciated," he said, sliding a twenty-cedi note through the man's fingers. Frank Dekker had told him earlier that day, "Nothing moves in this country without greasing a few palms."

The man felt the money, smiled, and tucked it discreetly into his pocket. "Don't worry, sah, I'll make—"

He was back to snoring loudly and Agent Hughes could do nothing but stare in utter bewilderment.

THE RAIN HAD subsided when Agent Hughes exited the *Daily Graphic* office. An old police squad car was waiting for him. It was the only support the Ghana Police Service had offered him after verifying his credentials.

"Where to, sah?" Officer Opoku asked Agent Hughes as he turned the key in the ignition.

"Back to the hotel."

"Yes, sah," Officer Opoku said, tipping his service cap. He had been sent to drive Agent Hughes around. But his real job was to keep an eye on his activities and report back to the Ghana Police Service. The drive back to the hotel was at rush hour and Agent Hughes was in no way prepared for the dense traffic. The bumper-to-bumper gridlock was so sedated that some drivers abandoned their vehicles in favor of a spirited game of draughts on the sidewalk. Agent Hughes felt the jet lag, and his eyelids weighed a ton. He passed out, and when he woke up the lights beaming from the hotel lobby blinded him.

"We're here, sah," Officer Opoku said as he pulled into the driveway.

Agent Hughes thanked him and strolled into the hotel foyer, where a few patrons were holding court. A man was adjusting the rabbit ears of a television near the bar, and Agent Hughes decided to get a drink and catch the news.

The static was thick, and the young female broadcaster's voice was barely audible. The bartender slid a bourbon across the table and wrote down his room number. As Agent Hughes sipped his drink he pondered his predicament with Fitzgerald and the Bureau. They had ripped him a new asshole over the phone, but he knew that apprehending Melvin and Bernadette would vindicate him. A small part of him had to admit, this felt like a John Petty déjà vu. Loud rapturous laughter snapped Agent Hughes back to himself. He glanced to see a heavyset man wearing safari shorts surrounded by a group of suit-wearing businessmen. As the laughter subsided, a thumping sound startled Agent Hughes. He turned to see Frank Dekker leaning against the bar.

"You sure move fast, old sport," he said with a smirk.

Frank Dekker slid a copy of the evening newspaper across the table, and Agent Hughes was surprised to see the headline: *FUGITIVE AMERICAN COUPLE HIDING IN GHANA.*

A photograph of Melvin and Bernadette appeared with the tip line and a one-thousand-cedi reward. Greasing a few palms certainly got things moving in this country, Agent

Hughes thought. He turned to Frank Dekker. "Are you staying here too?"

"Me? Never. Too many degenerates."

Frank Dekker gestured at the man wearing safari shorts. "You see that man? He's one of the biggest arms smugglers in the world. Don't ask me what he's doing here."

The man was Salvatore Costello, a notoriously shrewd businessman. During the Second World War he sold weapons to both the fascist government of Benito Mussolini and the British allied forces. Since then, he had been nicknamed *the Shadow,* because everywhere he went, a government was overthrown shortly after.

"There is no way I will be staying in the same hotel as that snake," Frank Dekker said as he shook Agent Hughes's hand. He walked to the corner of the lobby where a man wearing a large hat sat quietly. His name was General Kotoka, and he was Ghana's highest-ranking military general.

THE WULENSI TRAIN station had seen better days. The dilapidated roof did little to shield them from the pelting rain. Melvin nursed a blister under his foot as Bernadette wrung out her rain-drenched hair. They had waded through the knee-high water that flooded the dirt road leading to the train station. For an hour, they splashed and stumbled through the flood. Kwesi glanced back to see his American guests struggling to keep up. He wondered why they were so eager to get to Kulungugu with him. Maybe they were the adventurous type. He had read about foreigners like them in the newspapers, often mauled by some wild animal or robbed by bandits. They were always European tourists, never Negro evangelicals. And even if he thought to question their zest, Bernadette was prepared to charm him into oblivion.

THE FILTHY LAVATORY on the train platform reeked of death and decay. That was where Melvin, Bernadette, and Kwesi took turns changing into dry clothes. They heard the grinding sounds of a locomotive engine and Kwesi yelled, "It's coming!"

Melvin was back in a waspish mood and Bernadette tried to placate him.

"We're almost there, Mel," she whispered while nestled over his shoulders.

The speeding train made no indication of stopping, however. Flustered, Kwesi turned to Melvin and Bernadette. "We have to jump!"

They ran alongside the train, flung their bags into the open car, and leapt. Kwesi first, then Bernadette. Melvin missed the first car and hobbled his way onto the second. He attempted to join Kwesi and Bernadette through the door that connected the train cars, but it was locked.

"You okay, babe?" Bernadette shouted through the steel doors, her voice drowned by the oscillating pistons. Melvin propped himself feebly on the seat, lit a cigarette, and yelled, "Yes, babe. I'm fantastic."

THE GRAY EVENING mist obscured the rain droplets that rattled the train windows. Melvin tried to get some sleep, but his mind was fogged by thoughts of Kwesi and Bernadette alone in the next car. He wondered what they were up to. He could have sworn Kwesi was staring lustfully at Bernadette when she climbed aboard the bus that morning. And she had been way too cozy with him since the journey began. Sure, she'd said it was worth having him on their side, but was it *their* side or *hers*? What if he caught them in the act? Melvin knew Bernadette had never betrayed him, though the stress of their circumstances had brought out another side of them both. He stood, swayed from side to side, and peeked through the crevice of the metal door. He adjusted his eye until he saw Bernadette and Kwesi, fast asleep on opposite ends of the car. Melvin sighed deeply. All he had to do was survive one more day. After he reunited with President Nkrumah, he'd have no use for Kwesi and their paths would never cross again.

THE PHONE RANG twice before Agent Hughes jolted awake. He stretched his hand for the light switch but only found air. Then he tapped his way around the room until he felt the phone receiver. "Hello. Yes, this is Hughes. You're in the lobby? Okay, I'm coming down now."

Agent Hughes stared at the hydraulic elevator blinking from 4 to 3 to 2 to 1.

Ding!

He rushed out to find Officer Opoku waiting at the reception desk. The lobby was deserted except for an Indian couple waiting for their taxi to the airport.

"They sure had the misfortune of booking their flight at an ungodly hour," Agent Hughes sighed, as he slammed the police car door shut. The rain had dwindled to a light mist and Officer Opoku flicked the wiper control to clear his view.

"So the receptionist called the tip line?" Agent Hughes asked.

"Yes, sah, she recognized their photographs in the newspaper."

"I knew it," Agent Hughes said, pounding his fist.

OFFICER OPOKU PULLED into the Sea View Hotel driveway after thirty minutes. The front desk receptionist was in a sanguine mood. Her tight braids still seemed to stretch her large eyes apart.

"Yes, sah, that's them," she said, handing the photographs back to Agent Hughes.

"You're sure?"

"Absolutely," she replied, pointing at the spiral staircase that wrapped around the *SEA VIEW HOTEL* neon sign.

"They left through the balcony. Our cleaning lady saw them. They even left these—"

The receptionist pulled out two American passports and handed them to Agent Hughes.

He examined the passports intensely and stuffed them in his pocket.

"Did they say where they were going?"

"No, sah. But I told the man about Cape Coast, and he seemed interested."

"How far is Cape Coast?" Agent Hughes turned to Officer Opoku.

"Four hours, but in the rain? Five."

"You've been very helpful," Agent Hughes said as he slid his Bureau card across the reception desk. "If they come back, please call this number."

The receptionist sucked her teeth. "And what about my reward?"

She pulled out the newspaper from under her desk. "It says here, sah, one thousand cedis. So where is my reward?"

"If the information leads to their arrest." Agent Hughes pointed out the phrase in the newspaper. "We have to arrest them before I can pay you the reward."

The receptionist sank into her swivel chair and folded her arms. "Okay, then fifty cedis for the passports. That is my last price."

Agent Hughes knew an argument was futile, so he paid the receptionist fifty cedis and turned to Officer Opoku. "Cape Coast it is."

CHAPTER 11

The train pulled into the Yendi station after three hours. The bustle had just begun when the locomotive belched, hissed, and stuttered to a stop. Melvin leapt up, glancing out the window at the faces obscured by the predawn light. Most were market women hauling sacks of vegetables across the platform. Melvin remembered that Bernadette was in the next car with Kwesi. He quickly grabbed his shoulder bag and squeezed past a vendor as he climbed into the next car.

Kwesi and Bernadette were laughing hysterically when Melvin walked in. The excitement instantly deflated and Bernadette slid back to make space for Melvin.

"Sleep well, babe?"

"Nope, them seats was shit," Melvin said coldly as he lit a cigarette. He took a long drag. "How long is this stop?"

Kwesi shrugged. "I'm not sure. Maybe ten minutes?"

Three men dressed in identical gray suits and sunglasses climbed aboard the train. They carried a red suitcase and sat together in one row of seats. The men gave Melvin the creeps, an inexplicable sense of doom. The hissing sounds of pistons resumed, interrupting Melvin's malevolent thoughts. Kwesi excused himself and walked toward the restroom.

Melvin checked to make sure he was gone, then asked, "What were y'all laughing about?"

Bernadette chuckled. "Oh, nothing. Just Kwesi and his crazy stories."

"I see what he's trying to do, Bern, I know you see it too."

"What's he trying to do, Mel? Tell me."

"I don't trust him," Melvin sneered. "You don't think he's gonna flip on us the minute he know what we done?"

"No, Mel, you just paranoid is all."

An old ticket agent entered the train car. His oversized uniform, drab and frayed at the ends, hung shabbily over his lean frame. He tipped his hat, stretched his withered hand, and asked, "Tikiti?"

"No ticket, sorry," Melvin said, as he flicked the ash from his cigarette.

The old man hovered in the aisle until Kwesi returned from the restroom. They spoke in low tones, as if bargaining, and then Kwesi reached for his wallet.

"Just tell us how much," Melvin scoffed.

"It's ten cedis for all of us. I can pay for this and you pay for the next."

"No, you can pay for yourself. I'll pay for us two."

Bernadette shot Melvin a look, embarrassed. He ignored her, counted twenty cedis, and shoved it in the old man's hand. "Keep the change."

THE REST OF the train ride was spent in silence. Kwesi pretended to practice his guitar with muted notes. Melvin, wallowing in an air of indignation, stared out the window observing the landscape change from lush savanna to arid pastures. Bernadette slid to the corner of the seat and pulled out her diary. Then she inscribed the date in cursive:

January 6th, 1966

It feels like a never ending odyssey,
yet it's only been three days on the road.
A thunderstorm like I have never seen before,
forced us to change from a bus to a train.
Mel's attitude has gone from bad to worse.
Sometimes, I wonder how long I can put up with all of
*   this.*

Can't believe how naive I was, thinking Mel had all the
*   answers.*
On a positive note, we are meeting President Nkrumah
*   today.*
I have to admit I'm very nervous.
What if he refuses to help us? What happens then?
Mel hasn't considered that and I'm afraid to bring it up,
lest his anger flares again. All in all,
I am hopeful today and thankful for clarity.

The train screeched to a halt at the Bawku station after thirty minutes. It was the last stop for passengers traveling up north. The three men dressed in gray suits and sunglasses grabbed their red suitcase and brushed past Melvin. No apologies or acknowledgment. When Melvin turned, they had disappeared, lost in the crowd of vendors and herders.

Kwesi, growing nervous about his impending solo performance for President Nkrumah, led Melvin and Bernadette to the taxi rank. Drivers jostled for the few passengers who assembled at the station.

"I get air-condition for my car inside," one driver yelled.

"Ebi my car wey get radio for inside," another boasted.

Kwesi, overwhelmed by the chattering, walked up to a 1964 Fiat Coupé, which looked brand new. "Who car be this?" Kwesi asked, gazing at the disappointed faces.

Much to their displeasure, they called a young man who was sitting leisurely under a tree. He walked up and wiped his hands on his pants. "My car be dat. Where you dey go?"

"Kulungugu," Kwesi replied.

AGENT HUGHES STAYED awake for the entire five-hour drive to Cape Coast. Maybe it was the jet lag or the frightening thought that Melvin and Bernadette might have seen themselves in the newspaper and fled Ghana already.

"Do you need to use the toilet, sah?" Officer Opoku asked as they drove past a Shell petrol station.

"No, I'm fine. How much longer?"

"Thirty minutes, maximum."

THE EARLY-MORNING DRAB had given way to a luminous day when they arrived at Paradise Hotel. The bald-headed man behind the reception desk raised Melvin's and Bernadette's photos to the light. "Yes, that's them. The man is a pastor, right?"

Agent Hughes shook his head, confused.

"He said he was a pastor, even had the pastor thing around

his neck. He told me he would bring their passports down, up till now, nothing."

"So, they checked in without identification?"

"Yes, sah, but please don't tell my boss. I only did it because I go to church, you know, and I thought he was a pastor."

"And you didn't see them leave?" Agent Hughes asked, sliding the photographs back into his jacket.

"No, sah, I went to their room to ask about the passports again, and they were gone."

"Okay, I'd like to see your guest ledger."

The bald man agreed begrudgingly and disappeared into the back office. As Agent Hughes waited, he glanced at the reception desk decorated with knickknacks. A miniature plane, a wooden canoe, a game of Ludo, and a bamboo horse. At the far end of the counter was a worn-out globe of the world. It caught Agent Hughes's eye and he felt a palpitation ricochet through his chest. He grew light-headed and staggered backward. Officer Opoku, sensing an imminent collapse, helped Agent Hughes to a couch in the middle of the foyer. He swallowed a pill and it calmed the spasmodic throbs. He remembered that he owned a similar globe. It must have been his tenth or eleventh birthday gift from his father, Leo Pawlowski. The damn thing was supposed to bring happiness but it only caused him misery. His father, a strict Polish immigrant, quizzed him every night about continents, countries, and capital cities. Failure to answer a question resulted in a violent thrashing.

That was how the rift between Agent Hughes and his father began. It only worsened when Agent Hughes decided to join the FBI. The news upset Leo Pawlowski, who had been a lifelong communist. "You can't trust a country that will sell out its own people for profit," he said while sipping a glass of Polish Wódka Wyborowa. "You have failed me, Mikhail."

Those were the last words his father said to him before he emigrated back to Poland. Shortly after that, Agent Hughes changed his last name from Pawlowski to Hughes, after the great American business magnate and aviator Howard Hughes.

THE BALD-HEADED RECEPTIONIST looked down at Agent Hughes, propped feebly on the couch. "Here is the ledger, sah," he said reluctantly. Officer Opoku was busy fanning Agent Hughes with a magazine to curb the humidity.

"You don't look good, sah. Can I get you some water?" the receptionist asked.

Agent Hughes nodded, sat up straight, and began scrutinizing the guest ledger.

THE TAXI SPED down a narrow road as the tension between Melvin, Bernadette, and Kwesi seemed to thicken. Kwesi, overwrought and pensive, pondered some inconsistencies he had inadvertently overlooked. Like Bernadette's story about their Christian missionary work in Ghana. He couldn't fathom Melvin leading a church. He had neither the empathy nor temperament for a man of the cloth. Not to mention how much he smoked, drank, and cussed. Kwesi had given him the benefit of the doubt because he knew some missionaries who were equally discordant. But he had to admit, his growing infatuation for Bernadette was the reason he had been so blinded.

"How much longer is the drive?" Melvin asked.

"About fifteen minutes," Kwesi replied, checking his watch. "If everything is on time, we should have an hour before President Nkrumah arrives." The uncomfortable silence persisted and Kwesi felt compelled to fill the void with small talk.

"This has not been an easy journey, even for me. I can imagine how tired you are." His gaze shifted from Bernadette to Melvin and back.

"I guess you don't have to rush back for your missionary work?"

Bernadette shot Melvin a glance. He didn't even pretend to care, so she chimed in. "We have plenty of time, Kwesi. Our missionary work doesn't begin for another week, so thanks for letting us tag along. This is the authentic Ghanaian experience we were hoping for, right, Mel?"

Melvin shrugged. "Yeah, sure." Then he lit a cigarette, much to the driver's vexation.

"I beg, sah, this is genuine leather seat. No smoking in car."

Melvin ignored him and just kept puffing away. Bernadette gazed out the window, hoping her response satisfied Kwesi. For the first time in a while, she felt genuinely hopeful. They had made it this far up north to meet President Nkrumah, and she wanted to believe that their troubles were almost over. As the taxi approached the town square, Bernadette noticed the predominantly Muslim women wearing colorful hijabs and kaftan wraps. They reminded her of Ella. She was certain that Ella would have heard the news by now. The shooting, the daring escape, and her fugitive status in God-knows-where. What would she make of it all? Ella would sympathize with her, of course. If anyone would understand, it would be Ella. She just had a knowing about her. Bernadette touched her belly. She still wondered how Ella knew she was pregnant.

Bernadette decided that if she had a baby girl, she would name her Ella, because *Ella* meant "goddess," and what a fitting name for this child kept alive through so much turmoil.

Bernadette noticed the hand-painted patterns on mosques in Kulungugu. The beguiling contrast between the northern and southern territories was evident. The buildings in the north had a circular structure, unlike the angular buildings in the south. The topography was also distinct. The northern territories were arid and dry, while the south was lush and verdant. Amid her dilemma, Bernadette took a moment to absorb the beautifully diverse landscape, and she wondered how different her experience would be if she weren't a fugitive in Ghana.

THE TAXI PULLED up to the Kulungugu lodge at approximately ten A.M. Many of the renovations in anticipation of the president's arrival were complete. The painters were putting finishing touches on the exterior mud wall, and the lodge owner paced anxiously, overseeing their work. It was no secret that Baba Mumin disliked President Nkrumah. But he was a shrewd businessman, so he jumped at the opportunity to host Nkrumah's first northern gala. He was a tall, lanky fellow with tribal marks etched across his face. He flicked his Muslim prayer beads in his hands and occasionally stopped to adjust his oversized smock. He'd won the initial bid because he had a dreadful stutter and none of the other lodge owners had the patience to listen to him stutter through the bid session.

"Wel—Wel—, Wel—Welcome, Mist—Mist—Mister—Kwes—Kwesi Kway—Kway—Kway—Kway—Kway—Sorry—Kwayson," Baba Mumin said after the taxi eased to a stop.

He looked at Melvin and Bernadette in the back seat and stammered some more, "This—This—This—This is not your ba—ba—ba—ba—ba—"

"No, they are not my band," Kwesi interjected, which only irritated Baba Mumin.

"Wha—Wha—Wha—Wha— What happened," Baba Mumin asked in a deflated tone.

"The rain," Kwesi said, pointing to the sky. "My band was stuck in the rain. I had to come alone."

Kwesi couldn't bear any more of the conversation, which was progressing at a snail's pace. He grabbed his guitar case and asked, "Where is the stage?"

Baba Mumin didn't bother wasting his precious words on Kwesi. He just pointed at a banquet hall tucked behind an arched doorway and motioned Melvin and Bernadette toward the lodge.

The rooms were small and modestly furnished. The mud walls and bamboo fixtures added to the quaint décor. It was the type of place likely to be featured in an exotic travel magazine. The lodge had its downsides, however. Bernadette turned the shower knob and all she got was a rumbling sound. Not a single drop of water. Melvin was finally upbeat. He walked up to Bernadette and took her hand.

"In an hour, Nkrumah will be here and our nightmare will be over."

Bernadette smiled, allowing herself to be consumed by Melvin's optimism. He wrapped his arms around her. "I can't wait for him to meet you, Bern. Y'all will get along. I'm sure of that."

A knock shook the bamboo door. It creaked open and a

young woman hauling two buckets of water hobbled in. "For bath," she said, as she placed the buckets in the bathroom.

Bernadette bathed first, squatting over the frigid water. Each splash sent her body into shock and she murmured to herself, "It's almost over."

It was Melvin's turn to bathe and he cursed loudly each time the water touched his skin. Bernadette shivered under a frayed towel. She glanced and caught her naked reflection in the cracked mirror. Then she rubbed her belly gently and felt a slight bump. An air of serenity descended on her now that their grueling journey was coming to an end. She thought about how her baby would grow up knowing nothing about their ordeal. Perhaps she would write her story someday, but for now, she was just thankful that no harm had befallen them. Bernadette heard the bathroom door squeak open and she hurriedly wrapped herself in the towel to hide the tiny baby bump. Melvin walked in, shivering from the cold water. He dried himself, threw on his pastor's attire, and parted his hair neatly in the mirror. In spite of their circumstances, he was determined to look presentable to his best friend Nkrumah. Melvin checked his watch. They still had thirty minutes before the president arrived.

"You hungry, babe?" he asked Bernadette.

She nodded. "I can eat."

A LARGE BANNER billowed on the stage, with the words *WELCOME PRESIDENT NKRUMAH*. Kwesi was pacing through the hall anxiously when he saw Melvin and Bernadette. "Is there a good place to eat around here?" Melvin asked Baba Mumin.

"It's—It's—It's—It's—It's next door," he replied.

Bernadette walked up to Kwesi. "How are you feeling?"

He smiled. "Very nervous."

"You have performed for the president before, you will do fine," Bernadette said.

Then Melvin yelled from across the hall, "Let's get some food, Bern."

A CROWD HAD started to gather in anticipation of President Nkrumah's arrival. A few press cameras were setting up, and vendors jostled for space outside the lodge. They sold cheap souvenirs, trinkets, and anything that they could fit President Nkrumah's face on. Some genius had even figured out how to bake the president's likeness into loaves of bread. Melvin and Bernadette cut through the crowd in search of the restaurant. Then Melvin saw the three dreadful men still wearing their gray suits and sunglasses. They no longer carried the red suitcase, but they remained vaguely menacing.

Melvin shuddered and quickly turned away from them. He wanted to tell Bernadette about the men but didn't want to worry her more. For what? Their ordeal was almost over.

THE RESTAURANT WAS a wooden structure covered with tarp. The proprietress, Hajjia Assibi, kept a steady stream of patrons, which quickly stirred up rumors of witchcraft. Outlandish stories circulated about how a powerful fetish priest had turned Hajjia's two children into snakes, which gave her food a succulent aroma. But anyone who knew Hajjia knew that both her children were in boarding school in Accra, though that didn't stop the slanderous gossip.

"You want tuo zaafi, waakye, or jollof?" Hajjia asked.

Bernadette chose jollof, and Melvin, as he always did, opted for the same. Hajjia offered them palm wine, which Bernadette found nauseating. Melvin chugged his calabash and turned to Bernadette. "I'm gonna make it up to you, Bern, I promise. Once Nkrumah helps us settle, you wanna have that wedding we was planning?"

Bernadette was lost in thought. The wedding. The one she planned to have her friends and loved ones at, the one where Ella would be by her side in lieu of Ma' Susan. That wedding no longer existed. She knew deep down that nothing would ever be the same. In so many ways, she had seen a side of Melvin that felt irreconcilable. He was trying, sure, but would it be enough? In contrast, Bernadette had met Kwesi and she couldn't fully ignore that night. Had she imagined it, their bodies propelled above his bed, the magic she'd found hard to describe? Kwesi was the kind of man she'd known Melvin to be when they first met. She had to stick with Melvin, for now. She didn't want to throw away their years, but his actions had tried her more than she'd ever imagined. She would have to reassess everything after they gained asylum in Ghana.

Melvin asked again, "Bern, you wanna have that wedding we was planning?"

"Sure, Mel," Bernadette replied.

A GENERATOR ECHOED in the distance, and the stage lights illuminated. Kwesi glanced around the empty hall and brimmed with excitement. This was finally his moment. No backing band. No distractions. Just him and his guitar. President Nkrumah would be captivated and undoubtedly select him for his North America trip. Kwesi's dream was finally within reach. He decided to do a sound check before joining

Melvin and Bernadette at the restaurant. The amplifier blared through the hollow space as he fiddled his usual arpeggio. Then suddenly a dark insidious mist billowed from the guitar. When Kwesi looked down, he saw an inferno consuming the flower petals that bloomed out of the amplifier. The hall was soon swirling in a fiery combustion of burning flowers that disintegrated into ash in midair. Kwesi gasped and choked. He slowly lost consciousness, almost asphyxiating. Just as his world turned dark, Kwesi summoned his last bit of energy and yanked the cord out of the guitar. The inferno disappeared and Kwesi could breathe again. He coughed violently, spewing phlegm and saliva. His eyes burned, and his vision was hazy. As he lay prostrate on the hardwood floor, he decided to tell Bernadette what had happened. She was the only one who knew about the magic of his guitar, and he needed to decipher this omen. Kwesi floundered to his feet and walked toward the swarming crowd. A group of vendors selling beer and newspapers hassled Kwesi to buy one. He brushed them off and just as he turned, he caught the photographs of Melvin and Bernadette emblazoned on the front page of the *Daily Graphic*.

Kwesi stopped dead. His senses still overwhelmed, he rubbed his eyes and read the headline: *FUGITIVE AMERICAN COUPLE HIDING IN GHANA.*

He quickly paid for the newspaper and began to scan through the article. Suddenly, a loud commotion broke out in the crowd, followed by a chorus of sustained car horns. Kwesi turned to see the presidential motorcade, flanked by hundreds of Nkrumah supporters.

Melvin and Bernadette had just finished their meal when

they too heard the celebration. They paid Hajjia, rushed out, and saw the man, the myth, the enigma—Kwame Nkrumah.

He was standing atop the sunroof of his presidential limousine. He waved a white handkerchief and grinned widely. Melvin took Bernadette's hand and smiled. "Our savior is finally here."

Bernadette gazed in awe of Nkrumah. The adoring crowds chanted his name fanatically. They stumbled over each other, hoping to touch the hem of his garment. The limousine pulled up to the front of the lodge and President Nkrumah stepped out to rapturous applause. As was customary, the local administrators presented him with a bouquet of flowers. A little girl carried the bouquet elegantly to the motorcade, and as she approached Nkrumah, a loud ticking sound reverberated, and time seemed to stand still. All eyes were fixed on the little girl and President Nkrumah. Then a vicious, deafening explosion pierced the air.

PART 2

CHAPTER 12

The aftermath of the bomb left five people dead, thirty-four seriously injured, and the president of Ghana in the emergency room. Melvin's and Bernadette's ears were still ringing when they stumbled toward the lodge. Bernadette's primary concern was the safety of her baby. She kept her hand pressed against her womb and was relieved to feel a slight movement. When they arrived in their room, Kwesi was seething in the bamboo chair. His arm was soaked in blood from a shrapnel cut. He flung the newspaper at Melvin and screamed, "Liars, both of you."

Melvin and Bernadette stared at their photos on the front page of the *Daily Graphic* in utter bewilderment.

"You wanted to see the real Ghana, huh?"

"We can explain everything—" Bernadette started to say, but Kwesi cut her off.

"Why did you come here with me? Really."

Melvin pulled out the picture of him and Nkrumah standing in front of the Phi Beta Sigma banner. "He was my best friend. He would have helped us."

Kwesi gazed at the photograph as police sirens wailed in

the distance. He grabbed his guitar. "Well, you are on your own now. Good luck."

Kwesi stormed out the door and Bernadette instinctively gave chase. She caught up with him in the courtyard. "Kwesi, I'm sorry, we weren't honest."

"Honest? You killed a man."

"A white man who was part of a racist mob. He was going to hurt us. That's the truth."

The police sirens were fast approaching and Bernadette was at her wits' end.

"We need your help, Kwesi."

Kwesi would look back on this day and wonder why he didn't just walk away. It was his infatuation with Bernadette; he wanted to believe her, they'd been in harm's way and defended themselves. So, against his better judgment, he said, "Your face is in the newspaper. Nkrumah is in the hospital. You will have to leave the country now."

"We don't have our passports, that's the problem," Bernadette said.

Kwesi sighed, pondering an idea.

"I know a guy in Cape Coast. He can help."

Bernadette hugged him, tightly, affectionately. Melvin parted the curtains and saw their embrace. He sank slowly into the bed.

AGENT HUGHES AND Officer Opoku had just arrived in Accra when news of the Kulungugu bombing blared on the radio.

"It must be the coup plotters," Officer Opoku said.

"How do you know for sure?"

"Well, sah, this is the second time they have tried. I was there the first time."

Officer Opoku dug out a newspaper clipping from his glove compartment and handed it to Agent Hughes. "That's me right there," he said, pointing at his photograph in the newspaper.

"Go ahead, read it."

Agent Hughes raised the faded newspaper to the light.

THE CHRONICLE

July 7th, 1965

President Nkrumah survived the assassination attempt when a flock of birds descended on the Flagstaff House. The birds transformed into humanoid soldiers carrying Kalashnikov rifles. They swept President Nkrumah into the air and carried him to the hospital. When the coup plotters saw the SSV soldiers flapping their wings over the Flagstaff House, they surrendered instantly.

"What the fuck is this? That's not a real newspaper article." Agent Hughes laughed hysterically. "You people have wild imaginations in this country."

"Not imagination, sah. Everybody in Ghana knows the SSV saved Nkrumah that day."

Agent Hughes realized it wasn't a joke. "What the hell is the SSV?"

THE SSV, ALSO known as the Shapeshifters Vanguard, was a secret army sworn to protect President Nkrumah. Their reclusive leader, Prof, was an eccentric alchemist. It was rumored that he served his soldiers an elixir that transformed them into the likeness of any animal they chose. The SSV grew in legend after they rescued President Nkrumah from the Flagstaff House.

Agent Hughes slid the newspaper back into the glove compartment and sighed. "Birds that magically turn into soldiers and rescue a president? Now I've heard it all."

THE POLICE CAR pulled up to the Ambassador Hotel around four P.M. Agent Hughes thanked Officer Opoku and hurried to the front desk.

"I think you have a guest waiting for you," the receptionist said, pointing at a chubby white man reading a newspaper in the lobby. His hair was slicked back, and his flaccid chin hung loosely. Agent Hughes's heart raced as he walked toward the man, timidly.

"You know who I am?" the man asked, without taking his eyes off the newspaper.

"No, sir," Agent Hughes replied.

"I'm the guy they send when things are fucked up." He tossed his card on the glass table. Agent Hughes picked it up and felt the embossed seal of the U.S. State Department. Then he read the name on the card: *CHUCK SULLIVAN. U.S. CONSUL. SPECIAL AFFAIRS.*

"You came here without permission from your superiors? You cause a ruckus in the newspapers? And you compromised my field agent?" Sullivan pulled out a KLM plane ticket from his breast pocket. "You will depart Accra on the next flight to Washington in forty-eight hours. In the meantime you have been ordered to stand down."

"But, sir, I'm close to—"

"Shut the fuck up!" Sullivan slammed the newspaper on the table.

"I didn't come here to ask."

He stood up and hobbled out to a black Chrysler parked in the driveway.

AGENT HUGHES PACED apprehensively when he returned to his hotel room. This was worse than the John Petty Cuba debacle, he thought. He would surely be fired for this. His father, Leo Pawlowski, would read about his failure as an FBI agent and feel vindicated. Agent Hughes couldn't bear the thought. He decided that he would continue searching for Melvin and Bernadette until his forty-eight hours were up.

THE TRAIN RIDE back to the south was languid. Bernadette slept for most of the journey, propped on Melvin's shoulder while he smoked quietly. Kwesi noticed that the light in Melvin's eyes had extinguished. He gazed at nothing in particular. At that moment, Kwesi felt a deep sympathy for him. He was beginning to grasp Melvin's pain, now that he knew that they were wanted fugitives and their only hope, Nkrumah, was in the hospital.

Kwesi winced, feeling the pain from the shrapnel that had torn through his arm. He parted the train curtains to see the locomotive pull into Kumasi, their last stop.

Melvin, Bernadette, and Kwesi continued their journey in a chartered bus to Cape Coast that night. They traveled along gravel roads that turned into asphalt and back to gravel. No words were exchanged between them for hours.

. . .

THE MORNING DEW had just begun to reflect the sunrise when the bus pulled into Cape Coast. "What be your last stop?" the young driver asked.

"Peacock," Kwesi replied.

The Peacock Guest House was the farthest away from town. It was built by a local businessman who hedged his bets on tourists willing to visit an obscure fort in the area. Kwesi decided the guest house was a safe place to hide. It was secluded and had a small reception desk carved into the wall. The faded beige doors, rusted light fixtures, and overgrown poolside revealed a place long past its prime.

The old man behind the desk had an amputated arm. He reminded Melvin of his father, which made him apprehensive. Ordinarily he would have declined to stay, but knowing his predicament, he yielded.

The rooms were drab and mildewed. The furniture was derelict. A bamboo bed. A table. A chair. A raffia mat, and a wooden mask hanging loosely on the wall. Bernadette flung the window open for some much-needed fresh air, and an army of mosquitoes flooded in. Kwesi took the adjacent room, and after settling in, he knocked on Melvin and Bernadette's door.

"Come in," Bernadette whispered.

Kwesi strolled in and leaned against the wall, stoic and pensive. He tucked his hands in his pockets, hiding the fresh bandage that wrapped his arm.

"Have you decided where you are going to go?" Kwesi asked.

"We were hoping you could help us with that," Melvin said, shooting Bernadette a glance.

"Can you recommend a place?" Bernadette asked with the

same casual tone one might use when inquiring about a restaurant or bar.

Kwesi dug out a cigarette, struck a match, and cupped the flame until he puffed thick smoke. "Liberia will be your best option," he said. "They speak English, and a ship leaves once a week."

Kwesi had heard about Liberia from Eddy Jones and the other American sailors he'd worked for. He explained how formerly enslaved Negroes founded Liberia. "You can blend in there easily."

"Liberia sounds good, right, Bern?" Melvin glanced at Bernadette.

"Yes, Liberia is perfect," she replied. "Thank you for everything, Kwesi. We won't forget this."

Kwesi extinguished the cigarette he had barely smoked on the doorframe. "I will work on your passports now." He stepped into the hallway and Melvin hurried behind him.

"Hey, just want to say thank you. I'll pay you well when this is all over."

Kwesi pretended he didn't hear Melvin and continued to his adjacent room.

BERNADETTE SAT ALONE, her mind drifting like a rudderless ship. Leaving for Liberia didn't give her much comfort. Was this to be her fate? Running from one country to another? Then she thought of what would have happened if she'd never fled Philadelphia with Melvin. She would probably be in jail by now. But this too was jail, a different kind, perhaps even worse.

Melvin returned to the room and reclined on the bed.

"Why you think he's helping us?"

Bernadette shrugged. "I don't know, Mel."

"He didn't seem to want my money."

"Well, perhaps, he's helping 'cos he's good people."

Melvin chuckled. "If there's one thing I know, it's that no one does anything 'cos they're good people. Everybody wants something—even Kwesi."

AGENT HUGHES BARELY got a wink of sleep that night. When he finally started to drift off, the clamoring sounds of trucks pulling into the warehouse woke him. He spent the early dawn hours crossing out names from the guest ledger. He assumed that at least one patron helped Melvin and Bernadette in Cape Coast, and he was determined to find out who. Then he heard a faint knock on the door. Agent Hughes crept up, flipped up the cover of the peephole, and squinted to see— Frank Dekker, as ostentatious as ever. Even at six A.M. his long blond hair, Hawaiian shirt, bell-bottom pants, and sunglasses looked exquisite.

He strolled in with a bottle of Jack Daniel's in one hand and a 45-RPM record in the other.

"I heard you was leaving, I came to say goodbye," Frank Dekker said, uncorking the bottle of Jack, which he took straight to the head. After a couple gulps, he wiped his mouth and offered it to Agent Hughes.

"Too early for me."

"Ah, too bad," Frank Dekker replied, tossing Agent Hughes the 45-RPM record. He caught it and gazed at the cover.

"What's this?"

"A parting gift, sorta. It's one of the guys you've been looking for."

Agent Hughes stared at the record sleeve:

KWESI KWAYSON and his DYNAMO BAND—MAMI WATA HIGHLIFE.

There was a photograph of Kwesi holding his guitar and smiling confidently.

"That's who's harboring your fugitives. Sucks it's too late to do anything about it," Frank Dekker said.

"And how'd you know this?" Agent Hughes asked.

"Well, let's just say I got an informant in the band. He said your suspects are disguised as missionaries. Now tell me if you ever heard of nigger missionaries before?" Frank Dekker chuckled.

Agent Hughes shook his head disapprovingly. He flipped the record sleeve and gazed at the photograph of the whole band. He pointed to each member, and when he got to T, Frank Dekker nodded. "That's him."

T HAD BEEN providing Frank Dekker with sensitive information since they met at the gala for Queen Elizabeth. Her Royal Highness's visit to newly independent Ghana was a much-publicized event. The highlight was a dinner dance at the State House with President Nkrumah. Kwesi's hit record "Mami Wata Highlife" had just exploded, and he was invited to perform. As was usually the case, Kwesi and T had an altercation during sound check. T stormed out of the state house to cool down. That was where he met Frank Dekker, uncharacteristically dressed in a tuxedo. He was speaking with a British secret service agent who was conducting a security sweep at the behest of the queen. Frank Dekker spotted T and offered him a light for his cigarette. That was the beginning of their relationship. T briefed Frank Dekker and his CIA counterparts about the band's performances for President Nkrumah. Exact locations, names of high-profile guests and Russian intelligence officers present. With that intel, Frank Dekker built his operation to overthrow President Nkrumah with the support of the British intelligence officials. So as Queen Elizabeth danced in President Nkrumah's arms that night and Kwesi played "Mami Wata Highlife" for his distinguished guests, no one would have guessed that a conspiracy to depose Nkrumah was already in the works.

CHAPTER 13

Kwesi knocked on the door of a bungalow tucked behind a grove. A flock of chickens scurried past an old Kawasaki motorbike parked in the yard.

"Who dat?" a voice shouted from behind the door.

"Ebi me oh," Kwesi responded.

A young man stepped out, wearing a wrap around his waist.

"Why I see you keep so?" he beamed cheerfully. His name was Ebo. Kwesi's best friend from elementary school. They exchanged an elaborate handshake and Ebo led Kwesi into a living room. The turquoise walls were a stark contrast to the quaint furniture, most of which was still wrapped in its original plastic. A miscellany of old and new objects were scattered around the room. A transistor radio. A winding gramophone. A set of china plates. Two earthenware pots. And hanging above them all was an ornately framed photograph of Ebo's father, Paa Kofi. The portrait was one of Kwesi's earliest memories.

Ebo's father, Paa Kofi, was a local legend. He worked for

the British colonial treasury until he was fired for assaulting his British supervisor. He took what he learned at the treasury and started forging colonial copper coins. His forgeries were so precise that the British administrators couldn't tell if they were real or fake. This was because Paa Kofi was stealing the copper from recently installed electrical wires. It was rumored that while he was stealing the wires one night, his ladder broke and he came crashing down from twenty feet high. Everyone thought he was dead, but Paa Kofi leapt up, dusted himself off, and strolled home. A week later, Paa Kofi slept too close to the edge of his bed. He fell off, broke his neck, and died instantly. Everyone at the funeral grappled with the fact that the same man who fell from twenty feet and lived fell from his bed and died. So, as Kwesi sat in Ebo's living room, gazing at Paa Kofi's portrait some twenty years later, he was still perplexed by that paradox.

"Where you go hide for?" Ebo asked, throwing on a shirt.

"I dey on road oh."

"Oh, we hear everything. 'Mami Wata Highlife' dey play everywhere. You force waah," Ebo said, handing Kwesi a cold Star beer.

He took a gulp and set the bottle on the table. "Ebo, ebi sake of passport I come here."

Ebo smiled and raised his bottle. "You come the right place."

Ebo unequivocally was the premier forger in all of Ghana. He continued his father's forgery legacy, moving on from fake copper coins to land titles, birth certificates, and passports.

"Wey country you dey search?" Ebo asked, pulling out a secret compartment in his couch.

"Americano. Man and woman. Same last name."

Ebo rummaged through a box stacked with an assortment

of passports—Great Britain, West Germany, USSR, United States, Yugoslavia, and even Rhodesia.

He had a network of receptionists who sold passports left behind by forgetful patrons like William Murphy and his wife, Cindy Murphy. They had been vacationing in Cape Coast and returned to Accra for their departure flight only to realize that they had left their passports at the hotel. When they called, the receptionist replied, "Sorry, sah, we didn't find it."

KWESI FLIPPED THROUGH the passports. "How much?"

"Usually ebi fifteen hundred dollars each. But sake of I know you, two thousand for both," Ebo replied. Kwesi nodded and they shook on it.

OFFICER OPOKU FLIPPED the Odeon gramophone open. It was his most prized possession, so transporting it to Agent Hughes's hotel room was nerve-racking to say the least.

"I can wait till you are done," he said, stepping back to admire the magnificent suede and brass contraption.

"Thank you for doing this," Agent Hughes said as he cranked the silver handle. He lifted the gramophone arm and dropped the needle delicately over the 45-RPM record. Soon the vibrant sounds of "Mami Wata Highlife" blared through the room. Agent Hughes gazed at the rotating vinyl as if through some mystical telepathy it would lead him to Kwesi and eventually to Melvin and Bernadette. He found the polyrhythmic shuffle of "Mami Wata Highlife" intriguing. But his stoic gaze, which lasted the entire three minutes and twenty seconds of the song, revealed no indication of enjoyment.

When it was finished, Agent Hughes grabbed the record

sleeve, pointed at T's picture, and asked, "Do you know this man?"

Officer Opoku squinted. "Oh, that's Tetteh, sah. Everyone calls him T."

Agent Hughes's eyes lit up. "You know him?"

"No, but he is always at the racecourse gambling."

Agent Hughes lifted the "Mami Wata" record and slid it back into the sleeve. The wheels of his mind were turning, fast. He knew that finding T would bring him one step closer to finding Melvin and Bernadette.

"When is the next horse race?"

"There is a race every other day," Officer Opoku said. "If you are lucky you might find him there today."

Agent Hughes thanked him and the officer disappeared into the hallway with his gramophone.

THE ACCRA RACE Course sat in the middle of the Labadi township. The large archway entrance was flooded with a mixed bag of characters. Wealthy Ghanaian socialites, European expats, local riffraff, and even clergymen. The green bleachers were packed to capacity. Agent Hughes had to squeeze through the riotous crowd to get to his seat. He had a clear view of the betting booth and thought if T was at the race he would certainly place a bet soon. The afternoon sun burned the back of his neck and he checked his watch. It was two P.M. and he grew nervous. His anxiety triggered his heart palpitations and he swallowed a pill, washing it down with a bottle of Coca-Cola. A loud announcement pierced the overhead speakers, welcoming the guests. The starting gate burst open, catapulting the horses into their lanes. The hysterical crowd cheered their picks, yelling in a chorus:

"Go Dr. Godspeed."

"Go Good Fight."

"Go Ashanti King."

"Go Thunderbolt."

Some patrons stared through binoculars, waving their betting tickets fervently. The jockeys rode past and the bleachers were swallowed in a dust cloud. That was when Agent Hughes spotted T, walking down the narrow aisle to his seat. He hurriedly squeezed past two women and sat next to him.

"Excuse me, sir, are you T?"

T glanced around suspiciously. "Who wants to know?"

"My name is Agent Hughes, I'm a friend of Frank Dekker."

"Is Frank here?"

"No, he told me I could find you here."

Then a loud mix of celebration and disappointment broke out as the horses crossed the finish line. The announcer's voice shook the overhead speakers. "Ashanti King has won the Accra Derby. Repeat, Ashanti King has won the Accra Derby."

T ripped up his betting ticket and yelled, "Shit, Dr. Godspeed!"

Agent Hughes waited for T to calm down, then asked, "Can I buy you a drink?"

KWESI KNOCKED ON Melvin and Bernadette's door with a soft tap. Ebo pranced nervously behind him. Kwesi was about to knock again when Bernadette opened the door. "It's Kwesi, Mel." Melvin emerged from the bathroom, still brooding.

"This is Ebo, my friend," Kwesi said.

Ebo didn't look up from his shoes.

"He has two American passports and he's willing to sell both for two thousand dollars."

Melvin lit a cigarette, his tenth stick of the day. "You have 'em on you?"

"Yes, sah," Ebo said, reaching in his pocket.

Melvin inspected the passports thoroughly. When he was satisfied he handed them to Bernadette. All they had to do now was memorize a few details about Mr. and Mrs. Murphy. Their address was 287 Bordwin Drive, Boston, Massachusetts. Their arrival date in Accra was November 14, 1965. Their passports had one additional stamp on August 10, 1964, in Cairo, Egypt.

"He would need half of the money now, and half when he delivers," Kwesi said, eager to get things over and done.

"And the photographs?" Melvin asked.

"I brought my camera."

"Okay, and how soon can he deliver?" Melvin turned his attention to Ebo.

"Next week, sah."

"Nah, that's too late."

"He's the best," Kwesi interjected. "You don't want him to rush and make a mistake."

"He's right, Mel," Bernadette chimed in.

Melvin reluctantly handed Ebo two crisp five-hundred-dollar bills. "That means we'll miss this week's ship to Liberia. So next week?"

"Yes, sah," Ebo said, finally confident enough to look Melvin in the eye. "I have for you next week, no problem."

MELVIN AND BERNADETTE took turns posing in front of a white bedsheet for their passport pictures. Melvin remained aloof and his photograph looked like a mugshot. Bernadette, on the other hand, smiled brightly and struck a regal pose, arching her back and turning her neck like a swan in total stillness. Her skin glowed from the light pouring through the window. As Kwesi adjusted the aperture of the camera, it was easy to see why a woman as gorgeous as Bernadette could make a man like Melvin so jealous.

MOST OF THE seats at the racecourse had emptied out by midafternoon. From where Agent Hughes and T sat, they could see the janitors sweeping up thousands of betting tickets that littered the stands. Faint highlife music seeped out of the overhead speakers, and the few jockeys in the galleria enjoyed a quiet drink.

"A Johnnie Walker and Coke for you," the young server said, as he placed the glasses on the table.

"Cheers." Agent Hughes raised his glass to T, who hadn't fully recovered from his betting loss. Agent Hughes pulled out Melvin's and Bernadette's photos and spread them on the table. "Frank Dekker said you know where they are?"

T smiled, his posture finally loosened.

"I knew those Americans were suspicious. What did they do?"

Agent Hughes lowered his voice to a whisper. "They are wanted suspects in a murder."

"Wow, murder?—I wouldn't have guessed that." T sipped his drink and continued.

"They joined us in Cape Coast. Kwesi said they were American missionaries, but I never believed him. On our way to Kulungugu our bus was stuck in the rain and they ended up taking the train with Kwesi. I heard after the bombing they returned to Cape Coast."

"Do you know where they might be hiding?" Agent Hughes asked.

"No, but I can find out, for a price." He beckoned Agent Hughes closer and whispered, "I think Kwesi wants to sex the man's wife."

"What?"

"Yes." T made a lewd gesture, gyrating.

"You're sure?"

"Very sure."

Agent Hughes emptied his glass, eyes fixed on the deserted racecourse. "Interesting," he murmured to himself.

ON HIS TAXI ride back to the hotel, Agent Hughes pondered what T had divulged to him. A love triangle between Kwesi, Melvin, and Bernadette could work in his favor. It was, however, difficult for him to concentrate. The taxi driver was listening to a football game between archrivals Asante Kotoko and Accra Hearts of Oak. From his crimson regalia, it was clear that the driver was a Kotoko fan. He contorted every time the commentary alluded to a near miss or a spectacular strike.

Agent Hughes tried to focus on his predicament. He wondered if he could even trust T. Anyone as avaricious as him could be compromised easily. And besides, he had volunteered all that information without verifying that in fact Agent Hughes knew Frank Dekker.

"GOOOOAL!!!" the driver yelled, pounding on the steering wheel. Asante Kotoko had scored and the other vehicles honked loudly. Some passengers leaned out of their cars waving red flags. Agent Hughes watched the rapturous excitement in disbelief. He was certain that Frank Dekker and the CIA were planning something big. Most likely a coup d'état. He couldn't help but empathize with the oblivious Ghanaians celebrating a football victory when their country was on the brink of collapse.

THE OLD MAN behind the reception desk dusted off an ancient typewriter with his good arm. He smiled and said, "The *R* key does not work, but I can sell it for a hundred cedis." It was a Remington model typewriter with nickel-plated fittings. Melvin paid for it and the old man threw in some extra paper for good measure.

BERNADETTE HAD SPENT the afternoon on the balcony restitching the hems of her dresses to hide the inevitable baby bump that was slowly growing. She was playing for time and reckoned the longer she could keep Melvin in the dark, the better.

She was taking a bath when Melvin returned carrying the mammoth typewriter. He was determined to write another letter to President Nkrumah even though his last two letters had received no reply. Melvin slid in a fresh piece of paper and adjusted the carriage lever. Ignoring the fact that he had no *R* key, he began to type.

> Janua y 9th 1966
> Cape Coast, Ghana

Dea   P esident Nk umah,
    I hope this lette finds you well. I hea d
about you   ecent incident in Kulungugu and

p ay you have fully ecove ed f om you
inju ies. As a matte of fact, I was in
Kulungugu when it happened. The ci cumstances
unde which I have a ived in you count y a e
complex and I won't wo y you with the
details. Howeve , I am in g eat need of you
help. It is a matte of life and death. I
  emembe you told me many yea s ago at Lincoln
Unive sity that wheneve I made it to Ghana,
to look you up. Well, I am taking you up on
that offe , and the need is u gent. This is my
thi d lette to you. I doubt my fi st two we e
delive ed successfully. I am in Cape Coast
staying at the Peacock Lodge. Again I hope you
have ecove ed and look fo wa d to hea ing
back f om you.

You F iend.
Melvin Johnson.

CHAPTER 14

It was late afternoon when Melvin sealed his letter and strolled into the lobby. He found the one-armed receptionist in an effervescent mood, dancing to a vibrant tune on the radio.

"Hello. You know where I can find a post office?" Melvin asked.

The receptionist paused dancing and took Melvin's letter. "Don't worry, sah, I will make sure this is mailed for you." He adjusted his glasses and read the address on the envelope.

"For President Nkrumah?"

"Yes," Melvin gloated. "He's a good friend."

The receptionist nodded solemnly.

Unbeknownst to Melvin, his son had been thrown in jail by President Nkrumah's government for conspiring with the coup plotters.

Melvin, oblivious to the receptionist's sudden change in disposition, asked, "Is there anywhere I can get a drink?"

The receptionist didn't look up from the envelope. "There is a palm wine bar just across the street."

Melvin thanked him and as soon as he was out the door,

the old man ripped his letter to shreds and threw it in the garbage.

THE PALM WINE bar was empty, except for a little boy wiping the tables. A neatly woven fence of palm fronds lined the walls, letting in just the right amount of light. The furniture was scant. A table. Two benches. A bamboo chair, which looked more decorative than functional. On the table was an assortment of calabashes. The boy ran to the back when he saw Melvin, and a large woman wearing a colorful headscarf emerged. Her name was Auntie Esi, and she was the propri-etress of the bar.

"Sit where you like," she said as she adjusted her scarf.

Melvin sat on the edge of the rickety bench and almost tipped over. A flurry of houseflies circled the palm wine pot, and Auntie Esi swatted them with a piece of fabric. She served Melvin a medium-sized calabash and he chugged it without taking a break. When he looked up, the bar had transformed into a vibrant, discordant assemblage of locals. Laughter erupted at the other end of the bar with spirited conversations that evoked boisterous hand gestures. The atmosphere re-minded Melvin of the juke joints in Philadelphia he used to frequent. Bernadette hated it when he drank excessively, but these were strenuous times and he allowed himself to wallow in his misery. When Melvin finally looked outside, the evening twilight had descended. He stood up, light-headed, and searched for his wallet. After five minutes and a handful of lint, Auntie Esi surmised that Melvin had no money. She whis-pered something to the little boy, and he took Melvin's hand, leading him toward the Peacock Guest House.

· · ·

BERNADETTE SAT ON the bed watching the mosquito coil burn ethereally. She had spent the early evening in bed, wondering what her baby would look like. Perhaps her striking features would be passed down, or maybe Melvin's dark skin would win the day. Either way, she knew her baby would be beautiful. She thought about their apartment in Germantown and it made her nostalgic. Bernadette unpacked her diary and flipped through her entries. Each page brought tears to her eyes. She never imagined that her life with Melvin would be such a roller coaster. Their serendipitous meeting at Mr. Lomax's bookstore, their first kiss at Martha's Soul Food Restaurant, their late-night strolls through Melvin's vacant lot, and that horrible night at Otto's Diner. God, not that horrible night. It had brought out a side of Melvin she wished she had never known. Bernadette closed her diary and wondered where he was at that late hour. Then decided she didn't care. She thought about checking in on Kwesi but decided against that too.

A soft tap on the door interrupted Bernadette's musings. She opened it slightly to see a little boy. Melvin was leaning against the wall, inebriated. The little boy held out his hand. "Sika?"

Bernadette searched through her purse and gave him a one-cedi coin. She had no idea if that was enough, but the little boy smiled and scurried away. Melvin brushed past Bernadette and crashed into the bed. She took off his filthy shoes, unbuttoned his shirt, and slid a pail next to the bed. She paced the small room, frustrated that Melvin had gone off and gotten drunk, as if he were the only one in turmoil. The room felt stuffy and the ceiling fan did little to curb the stifling heat. Melvin's loud snoring further irritated Bernadette, and she desperately needed some air. She threw on her floral kimono and stepped out of the room. Stopping by Kwesi's door, she put her ear close and heard him practicing. No, she wouldn't bother him. Bernadette continued through the corridor overlooking the courtyard and descended the stairs leading to the swimming pool, overgrown and obscured by a lush grove of mango trees.

She gazed at her reflection in the pool, and suddenly a cascade of ripples converged into a bright glimmering light. Bernadette felt a great force lift her into the air. When it let go, she splashed into the water and began to sink slowly. Bernadette couldn't tell if she was dreaming or awake, but she didn't resist. The water transformed into a vast ocean and she gazed at a flurry of flowers swirling in the distance. A silhouetted figure swam toward her. Bernadette blinked to see—Alice, her mother, in the form of a mermaid.

She looked regal, divine even. Her thick gray locs were shrouded in a halo of splendor. "My daughter," her voice thundered, "the ocean holds everything you seek. We belong to it and it belongs to us. We are known by many names: Yemoja, Yemanja, Mami Water, and thousands more." When Bernadette's eyes adjusted to the light, she saw the mermaid totem that Ma' Susan had bequeathed her floating in the water.

"You are here for a purpose," Alice thundered once more. "This is the land of our ancestors, those who survived the perilous journey across the ocean, thrown overboard and adapted to the water; we return to this land, to help free and be freed. One man holds the key, but he has lost his way, betrayed his destiny. But soon you both will realize yours."

Then Alice turned and swam toward the gleam. Bernadette

felt the same force lift her from the pool. She levitated until the beam disappeared and she floated back to the ground. Bernadette lay down momentarily, gathering her wits. Was she losing it? Had the stress taken her mind? She stood up, overwhelmed by the experience. She thought about her grandmother Ma' Susan, and the otherworldly story about the day she was born. It wasn't a mendacious fable after all. Then she thought of Kwesi and his story about the mermaid that rescued him. Was it Alice? Did she give him that guitar?

That night Bernadette tossed and turned until the morning sun crept through their window. When she woke up, she had the urge to tell Kwesi everything. Her encounter with Alice, their mystical bond, maybe even her pregnancy. She was desperate to tell someone, anyone but Melvin.

AGENT HUGHES WAS up before his alarm beeped at eight A.M. He packed his suitcase and ripped Melvin's and Bernadette's photographs off the wall. Then he checked his KLM ticket, verifying that his departure was at three P.M. That gave him six hours for T to call.

They had agreed at the racecourse that if T found out where Melvin and Bernadette were hiding, he would phone him. To pass the time, Agent Hughes had breakfast sent up. Two eggs, sunny-side up. Two sausage links. A cup of coffee. And a can of baked beans he never ordered. "Damn British," he murmured. It wasn't enough that they colonized half the world, they had to force their shitty baked beans on everyone too.

He finished his breakfast and there was still no word from T. As a last-ditch effort, Agent Hughes decided to call him. He unfurled the racecourse napkin with T's number scribbled in ink. Then he spun the rotary phone, held the receiver to his ear, and waited.

And waited.

Agent Hughes heard the high-pitched beeping sound and stopped dead. He had been trained to spot a bug in the Bureau, and he was certain that his phone was tapped. He hung up and parted the hotel curtains. Chuck Sullivan's black Chrysler was parked discreetly across the street.

"Dammit." He sighed.

BERNADETTE KNOCKED ON Kwesi's door with a faint tap. He opened it and peeked down the hallway, expecting to see Melvin too.

"He is still sleeping, hungover I suppose," Bernadette said.

Kwesi ushered her inside and sat in a bamboo chair.

"How are you feeling?"

"I'm all right. You know, can't wait for this to be over."

"I understand."

Bernadette hesitated. "I came to tell you something, Kwesi. I—"

A knock on the door interrupted Bernadette.

"Bern! You in there?" Melvin shouted.

Bernadette leapt to her feet. "Sorry, Kwesi, I have to go."

She opened the door and brushed past Melvin.

"What you doing in there?" he sneered. "I asked you a question, Bern. What you doing in there with him?"

"What? You don't trust me?" Bernadette yelled.

"I don't," Melvin replied, shutting the door behind them.

Suddenly Melvin grabbed her throat and slammed her

against the wall, his breath still reeking of palm wine. Bernadette choked and kicked, suffocating from his tight grip. Melvin, finally conscious of what he was doing, released her.

"I'm sorry, babe—I'm so sorry."

Bernadette slid down the wall, her eyes bloodshot.

"Get out, Mel! Get the fuck out!"

Melvin lowered his head and staggered into the hallway, disappearing into the morning mist.

BERNADETTE SOBBED QUIETLY on her pillow. She rubbed her belly gently, praying her baby was all right. Should she have told Melvin that she was pregnant? Would he have been violent with her if he knew?

Then a loud knock startled her. "I said, go away!" she yelled.

"It's me," Kwesi whispered.

"Kwesi?"

"Yes—can I come in?"

"One minute," Bernadette sniveled, wiping the tears running down her cheeks.

Kwesi stepped into the room, his eyes darting around the chaos until he landed on the bruise marks etched on Bernadette's neck.

"He did this to you?" Kwesi asked, bewildered.

Bernadette averted her eyes. "It doesn't matter now—"

Kwesi sank into the bed, pondered for a minute, and said, "We should run away. I know a place Melvin will never find us."

"Run?"

"Yes, you and me."

"I don't need saving, Kwesi, and I can't run anymore. I already did that with Melvin. I'm not following another man to God-knows-where."

At that moment, Bernadette was thinking only about herself and her baby. The life she would make for them, away from Melvin. Yes, her connection with Kwesi was undeniable and her encounter with Alice had reinforced their otherworldly bond, but Bernadette had to make a choice, and her mind was made up.

AGENT HUGHES CHECKED his watch as he waited for the elevator. It was about one-thirty P.M. He grabbed his suitcase when the doors parted and squeezed beside a young Ghanaian couple. They chuckled flirtatiously and Agent Hughes couldn't help but envy their blissfulness. The elevator arrived in the lobby and just as Agent Hughes stepped out, a young man with an Afro blocked his path.

"Hughes?"

"Yes," Agent Hughes replied.

"I'm Wilfred, your ride to the airport."

"Oh, I was just about to call a cab?"

"Don't worry, I got you."

Wilfred took Agent Hughes's bag rather forcefully and led him out of the lobby.

The afternoon sun beamed through the windshield and Agent Hughes adjusted his seat to avoid the glare. Wilfred turned the key in the ignition. "Hey, man, you know I'm just doing my job, right?"

"Of course you are," Agent Hughes replied, checking the side-view mirror. He had clocked Sullivan's black Chrysler tailing them.

"You like it here?"

"It ain't half bad, I just miss ma ol' lady is all."

AFTER TWENTY MINUTES on the road, the Land Rover pulled into the airport terminal. A police officer dressed in all white asked, "What airline, sah?"

"KLM," Wilfred said.

The officer motioned them toward the departure hall. Wilfred pulled over and shook Agent Hughes's hand firmly. "Good luck in Washington, you gonna need it."

THE KLM DEPARTURE lounge was crowded with mostly American and European passengers. A few Ghanaian citizens were waiting for their flights too. Agent Hughes felt anxious, wondering if T's calls had been intercepted. Surely, if the CIA had tapped his hotel room phone they could intercept his calls too.

A gate announcement blared out of the airport intercom. Agent Hughes pulled out T's phone number and walked up to the freckle-faced ticket agent at the KLM counter.

"Hello, sir, may I help you?" she asked in a thick Dutch accent.

"Yes, ma'am," Agent Hughes said. "You have a phone I can use?"

"Of course," she replied, placing the rotary phone on the counter.

Agent Hughes dialed T's number and waited—

"Hello. Yes, is this T?"

"No, this is the Abeka post office," a voice replied. "I can tell T to call you back."

"Yes, please have him call this number—" Agent Hughes

lifted the rotary phone and read the digits inscribed underneath. He hung up and turned to the freckle-faced ticket agent. "He's going to call me back."

She nodded politely and went back to punching numbers on her calculator.

Agent Hughes tapped his foot anxiously. His heart palpitations began to flare and he reached in his coat pocket for his medication. He was horrified to find only one pill left. He couldn't risk taking it now, he thought. Suddenly the shrill sounds of a ringing phone startled him. He leapt up and snatched the phone receiver.

"Hello? T?"

"Yes, sah. I called your hotel but your phone is not working."

"No worries, I'll explain later." Agent Hughes cupped the receiver and lowered his voice to a whisper. "Any news about the suspects?"

"Yes, I have confirmation that they are in Cape Coast."

"Can you meet me at the airport?"

"Now?"

"Yes—right now," Agent Hughes said.

CHAPTER 15

Melvin stared at his reflection in the misty palm wine residue. He was on his fourth calabash. The dirge-like melody on the transistor radio made him melancholic. He felt a deep remorse about his altercation with Bernadette. They had rarely quarreled, and even when they did, it never turned violent.

Melvin wondered what could have pushed him over the edge. Of course, the never-ending string of bad luck had something to do with it. He wasn't just losing himself, he was losing Bernadette too. He needed someone to be at fault, other than himself.

"Fuckin' Kwesi—" Melvin murmured.

He decided that Kwesi was to blame for all of this. They would have to get away from him once and for all. The ship leaving for Liberia tomorrow was their best bet. That meant Ebo would have to expedite their passports. Melvin walked up to Auntie Esi. "Excuse me, madam, do you know Ebo?"

She looked up, surprised that the American stranger had a question. "Tall Ebo or short Ebo?"

Melvin took a wild guess. "Tall Ebo."

"Yes, he lives just here. Fifi can take you now."

Melvin paid for his drinks and followed the boy through a maze of corrugated shacks. An ominous cloud had swallowed the sun, and the narrow path was barely visible. The boy pointed at a house tucked within a grove of almond trees. "Ebo," he said. Melvin thanked him with a coin and the boy scampered away.

Then he knocked on the door, hard.

Ebo swung it open. "Pastor, is something wrong?"

"No. Can I come in?"

"Yes, sah," Ebo said nervously.

Melvin sank into Ebo's couch with the plastic cover. "I need the passports tomorrow."

"But, sah—"

"I'll pay you an extra thousand dollars," Melvin interjected.

"I can make that work, sah."

Melvin leapt up and shook Ebo's hand. "You have to bring the passports to me directly, not Kwesi. You understand?"

"Yes. Bring passport to you tomorrow, not Kwesi."

Melvin strolled into the darkness, with a firm resolve to leave Ghana with Bernadette and never look back.

A SPLASH OF headlights blinded Agent Hughes as he emerged from the airport terminal. He was relieved to see T step out of a brand-new Renault Dauphine. He carried an umbrella that did little to shield them from the rain.

"Thank you for coming," Agent Hughes said, wiping his wet hands on his trousers.

T winked. "One hundred dollars a day. That is my fee. Non-negotiable."

"No problem." Agent Hughes dug in his wallet and handed him a crisp hundred-dollar bill.

T took the money and smiled. "This is why I like doing business with you Americans."

Agent Hughes rubbed his hands across the fine detailing of the Renault Dauphine. "Very nice car," he said.

T shrugged. "It's for my brother. He would kill me if he knew I was driving it. Where to?"

"*The Daily Graphic,*" Agent Hughes replied.

THE FLABBY GENTLEMAN behind the desk was snoring loudly. It had been thirty minutes and Agent Hughes had barely gotten a sentence in. It was déjà vu all over again. How the hell does a narcoleptic get a job at a major newspaper anyway?

Flustered, Agent Hughes kicked the man's leg from under the table and his jaw fell out of his hand, jolting him awake. "Sorry, sah. Did I fall asleep again?"

Oh, for fuck's sake, Agent Hughes wanted to scream, but he just nodded.

"You have still not arrested your fugitives?"

"No. I need you to print the story again."

"Same story?"

"Yes. Same reward and tip line."

The man exhaled contemplatively. "My editors will be expecting something to run this story again."

Agent Hughes nodded. "Yes, I know nothing moves in this country without greasing a few palms."

· · ·

THE WESTERN UNION office was Agent Hughes's next stop. A young lady was filing documents in a cabinet when he stepped inside.

"Hello, sir, how may I help you?"

"I need to send a telegram," Agent Hughes said.

The young lady handed him a pen and paper and he began scribbling. When he was done, he handed the paper to the lady.

"To Washington, D.C.?" she asked.

"Yes, ma'am."

The clicks of the telegram machine reverberated and then she held up the message for Agent Hughes to verify:

MR. JAMES FITZGERALD.

FEDERAL BUREAU OF INVESTIGATIONS.

WASHINGTON D.C.

JANUARY 10 1966.

I'M SORRY TO MISS FLIGHT. I HAVE DECIDED TO STAY
    IN GHANA

TO FINISH INVESTIGATION. WILL NOTIFY WITH FUR-
    THER DETAILS.

CABLE IF NECESSARY.

HUGHES.

"Do you want to wait for a reply, sir?" the young lady asked.

"No, ma'am," Agent Hughes said, bracing himself for another drive to Cape Coast.

❉

BERNADETTE WAS FAST asleep when Melvin returned from Ebo's house. He took off his shoes quietly and lay next to her, cupping her slender body.

"Kwesi. I can't—" Bernadette mumbled in a dreamy tone.

Melvin leapt up. His heart raced. Then he realized she was talking in her sleep. Thank God they were leaving tomorrow, far away from Kwesi and this godforsaken country.

THE MORNING LIGHT beaming through the large windows woke Bernadette. She turned to see Melvin sitting on the edge of the bed with a bouquet of flowers.

"I couldn't find no lilacs, babe. They ain't got 'em in this country," Melvin said as he handed her a bundle of bougainvillea. "I just want to say how sorry I am about yesterday. I don't know what came over me."

Bernadette sat up in the bed, clasping her arms and knees together. This was becoming a routine she loathed. Melvin's apologies and empty promises. Time was running out and she needed a plan of her own. But Bernadette couldn't raise any suspicions, so she just took the flowers and said, "Thanks, Mel, I hear you."

THERE WAS AN awkward silence at breakfast that morning. Kwesi, Melvin, and Bernadette barely exchanged any words. It didn't help that the one-armed receptionist served an insipid combination of bland eggs and dry bread. Bernadette's eyes were fixed on a cube of sugar dissolving slowly in a cup of Lipton tea. Kwesi kept his eyes on the bruise marks on Bernadette's neck. A quiet rage burned inside him. In that moment he decided he would give Melvin up to the police.

Yes, that would mean Bernadette would be questioned, but he would vouch for her. He would finally be alone with Bernadette, without Melvin hovering. His mind catapulted to their otherworldly kiss in his room. A kiss he had longed to relive since that night. They could leave Ghana, perhaps he could even go to America with her, after Melvin was arrested.

KWESI WAITED FOR Melvin and Bernadette to excuse themselves, and then he crept to the reception desk and dialed the police tip line.

A distant voice answered, "Hello, Ghana Police."

Kwesi was about to speak, and then he stopped short. Had he thought this through? Was he prepared for the consequences? What if Bernadette was arrested too?

"Hello, Ghana Police. You have a tip?" the voice reverberated again.

Kwesi hung up quickly, trembling with fear. Then he felt a hand grab his shoulder. He turned sharply to see—Melvin. His eyes darted from Kwesi to the phone and back to Kwesi.

"You okay?" he asked suspiciously.

"Yes—yes, I was just going to see Ebo about your passports."

"Okay, this is for you." Melvin handed him an envelope full of cash. "I told you I'd give you something when this was all over."

Kwesi thought about rejecting the money, but he was so spun out of his wits that he just took the envelope and hurried out of the guest house.

. . .

MELVIN PACED BACK and forth in the lobby trying to make sense of Kwesi's strange behavior. He could feel it deep down, something wasn't right. Suddenly, the telephone rang, startling Melvin. He grabbed the receiver and heard the same distant voice. "Hello, this is the Ghana Police, you called to report a tip?" Melvin's heart sank. He quickly hung up.

BERNADETTE WAS FOLDING her clothes when Melvin barged into their room.

"I told you we couldn't trust him," he barked.

"What the hell, Mel?"

"I told you he would turn on us, didn't I?"

"Who?"

"Kwesi! Who else?"

"What happened?"

Melvin paused and took a deep breath, "I went down to give him his money, you know, for helping us. He seemed tense, so I ask, what's going on, Kwesi? He says, oh, I'm just going to see Ebo, for the passports. So I say okay. He leaves, then the phone rings. Guess who?"

"Who, Mel?"

"Ghana—Fuckin'—Police. He called them to give us up."

Bernadette plunged onto the bed. "No, not Kwesi."

Melvin started to pace again. "I told you, Bern, I told you."

"Where's he?" Bernadette asked.

"Gone. Abandoned us."

Bernadette buried her face in her palms.

Melvin rushed to her side. "I'm sorry, babe. I'm gonna fix this. I promise." His tone was assured as usual. "We not leaving next week, Bern, we leaving today. I worked it out with

Ebo. He's gonna bring the passports directly to us, not Kwesi. I'm paying him a li'l extra, but we leaving today."

Bernadette wiped the tears from her eyes. She didn't know what to believe. Did Kwesi really call the police? Was Melvin making it up? She was reluctant to go to Liberia with him, but if Kwesi had in fact betrayed them, it wouldn't be wise to stay in Ghana. So she turned to Melvin and said, "Best to start packing now."

CHAPTER 16

The decrepit bottle factory sat idly in the center of Accra. The countless empty bottles on the conveyor belt seemed to crystallize time. Like Pompeii of old, shrouded in the ashes and mystery of a time long gone. That was where Frank Dekker headquartered his shadow operations for the CIA. He ran a skeleton crew of three highly trained agents sworn to never reveal what they did in Ghana.

Their makeshift office had a wooden table. Three chairs and two telephones. One was for outgoing calls. The other was for emergencies and was never supposed to ring. They kept no documents, no records, and no memos. The fire pit outside the warehouse contained the ashes of highly classified espionage.

A tattered calendar hung on the wall with the date circled in red permanent marker. Everything they had worked on for the last year came down to this day. Frank Dekker and his team reviewed the last salient documents that confirmed that Nkrumah was scheduled to travel to Hanoi today. The trip had been long planned. And even after the Kulungugu bombing, Nkrumah was still adamant about traveling to show his constituents a sense of normalcy. Frank Dekker scanned through a confidential memo Nkrumah had written to the U.S. president, Lyndon B. Johnson:

CLASSIFIED.

Dear President Johnson,

My special envoys brought me some information from Hanoi which I did not divulge to my foreign minister. President Ho Chi Minh has requested my presence in Hanoi and has proposed a cease-fire to ensure my safety. It is clear to me that the gap which divides the parties to the conflict in Vietnam is very narrow. I believe that with goodwill and patient effort, it will be possible to bridge this gap in order to lead to a negotiated settlement, and thereby ensure world peace.

President Nkrumah

"Who the fuck does he think he is? This nobody wants the president of the United States to cease hostilities so he can travel to Vietnam. I mean the balls on this guy!" Frank Dekker chuckled.

Frank Dekker knew that the situation only made his job easier. Agree to a cease-fire, get Ho Chi Minh to invite Nkrumah to Vietnam, and while he's gone, orchestrate a coup d'état.

Everything was going as planned, until the telephone that was never supposed to ring rang. Frank Dekker gazed at the receiver slack-jawed. His pulse began to race. Had his co-conspirator grown cold feet? Had the army decided it was too risky to attempt the overthrow? Everyone exchanged nervous looks as Frank Dekker answered the phone.

"Frank, we got a problem," Chuck Sullivan said. "That son of a bitch Hughes never got on his flight to Washington."

Frank Dekker sighed deeply. "You are sure of this, sir?"

"Am I sure? Fuck yeah, I'm paid to be sure. Hughes was spotted with your informant, T, driving to Cape Coast."

Frank Dekker sank deep in his chair. "I will see to this myself, sir."

"We can't allow Hughes to fuck this up, Frank. Do your damn job."

THE RENAULT DAUPHINE pulled out of Hotel Afriko around midday. It was the fourth hotel where Agent Hughes had inquired about Melvin and Bernadette since they arrived in Cape Coast. As he crossed it off his list, he felt a sharp pain in his chest. Agent Hughes had resisted taking his last pill, but he was beginning to feel light-headed from the throbbing pain.

"Are you okay?" T asked.

"I'm fine," Agent Hughes stuttered.

T didn't believe him, so he pulled into a Shell petrol station for a cup of water.

Agent Hughes swallowed his last pill and reclined in his seat.

"Do you want to take a break?" T asked.

"No!" Agent Hughes replied emphatically. He read out the name of the next hotel and T put the car in drive. They maneuvered through a stretch of dirt road until they encountered a massive herd of cows. The herdsmen casually strolled with sticks hoisted on their shoulders. T sighed. "See these Fulani herdsmen, they always block the road like they own it."

He turned on the radio to pass the time and a disc jockey's voice seeped out.

"This new act from Nigeria is going to be the future of African music. It is my delight to play you the brand-new single from Fela Ransome Kuti and His Koola Lobitos, 'It's Highlife Time.'" The funky horns blared out of the speaker.

T sucked his teeth. "Listen to this nonsense. It sounds just like 'Mami Wata Highlife.' Can you believe this?"

T waited for a response but got nothing. He glanced to see Agent Hughes snoring in the passenger seat, then cut off the radio angrily.

THE SUN BLAZED through the asphalt as the Renault Dauphine pulled up to the Ocean Hotel. The receptionist adjusted her thick glasses, scanning Melvin's and Bernadette's photographs.

"Yes, that's the American man and his wife."

Agent Hughes's eyes lit up. "They came here?"

The receptionist hesitated. "I can't share that information with you, sah."

Agent Hughes pulled out a twenty-cedi note.

She took the money hurriedly and whispered, "They are here right now. In room eight." Agent Hughes put his finger across his lip gently. Then he pulled out his Smith & Wesson service revolver. The receptionist, frightened at the sight of the gun, scurried behind the desk.

Loud laughter poured out of the room as Agent Hughes approached the hallway. He aimed his revolver, took a deep breath, and kicked in the door. A naked couple screamed and Agent Hughes stopped dead in his tracks. He realized they were neither Melvin nor Bernadette.

"I'm sorry, wrong room," he muttered.

"Get the fuck out of here, damn cracker," the man yelled,

as his lover hurled anything she could grab at him. Agent Hughes was unaware that he had interrupted a weekly rendezvous between an American Negro doctor and his Ghanaian secretary. He walked down the hallway, shoulders slumped.

"Was it them?" T asked excitedly.

"Nope." Agent Hughes shook his head. He read the name of the last establishment on his list—"Peacock Guest House."

KWESI PACED ANXIOUSLY outside Ebo's house. He needed a place to clear his head. Somewhere quiet and far away from Melvin and Bernadette. He knocked on the door and waited. Then he realized Ebo's Kawasaki motorbike wasn't parked in its usual spot.

Kwesi sat on a bench outside the house, pondering his predicament. How did he get entangled in such a dreadful mess? Then he wondered if Melvin knew that he'd called the police. What would Bernadette think if she found out? She would never trust him again. Then Kwesi remembered that his guitar was still in his room. It was his most prized possession and quite possibly his only true connection to Bernadette. He decided to wait until he was certain the police hadn't traced his call back to the Peacock Guest House. Then he would get his guitar and explain everything to Bernadette.

THE DEAFENING SOUNDS of a 707 aircraft thundered in the distance. Frank Dekker checked his watch again. It was three P.M. Nkrumah was scheduled to depart for Hanoi an hour ago. But his plane was still on the tarmac. Frank Dekker grew nervous, smoking a whole pack of Marlboros as he waited.

He lifted his binoculars and scanned the runway from his Peugeot. Then the roaring 707 engine rose in cadence, and the presidential jet sped down the tarmac and was soon airborne.

"About fuckin' time," Frank Dekker said, grabbing his walkie-talkie. He cleared his throat. "The falcon is in the air. Repeat. The falcon is in the air. Over."

His voice echoed out of multiple radios at the Accra military barracks where his co-conspirator, General Kotoka, waited. He was surrounded by his army of coup plotters, most of whom had orchestrated the Kulungugu bombing. This time they planned to get it right. General Kotoka leaned into the radio and announced, "Operation Cold Chop activated."

THE FIRST DEPLOYMENT of General Kotoka's soldiers was to the Ghana Broadcasting Corporation. They ambushed the studio and arrested all pro-Nkrumah journalists. The second deployment was to the armory. Soldiers loyal to Nkrumah fled their posts when they heard machine-gun fire in the distance. Armed with the arsenal of weapons, General Kotoka and his men ambushed the Flagstaff House. The presidential guards hadn't heard about the attack at the Ghana Broadcasting Corporation. So when a loud explosion shook the front gate, they were ill prepared. An hour-long gun battle ensued between the guards and General Kotoka's men. Grenades exploded and Kalashnikov shells ricocheted through the yard. When the smoke cleared, twenty members of Nkrumah's presidential guard lay dead. The entire operation took one hour, and President Nkrumah's government was overthrown.

CHAPTER 17

The humidity soaked through Melvin's pastor's collar. He paced anxiously, keeping an eye out for any police cars driving by.

"Have a seat, Mel, you're making me nervous," Bernadette said.

"Sorry, babe, you know we can't leave without our new passports."

"Well, Ebo said he'll bring 'em today, so let's just relax."

Melvin sank into the bed and caught his reflection in the mirror. He was dressed in the same pastor's regalia as the day they fled Philadelphia. Bernadette also opted for her now-loosened floral dress and large-brimmed hat. Their disguises had served them well and they needed them once more en route to Liberia.

A knock shook the door, and Melvin leapt up. "Who is it?"

"It's me, Ebo," a faint voice replied.

Melvin opened the door cautiously and Ebo rushed in.

"You have not heard the news?"

"What news?"

"The coup d'état? They overthrow President Nkrumah's government just now."

Melvin's jaw dropped. "No—it can't be true!"

"Yes, sah, it just happened now. Military everywhere. The ship leaves in one hour, sah. You must go now."

Ebo handed Melvin the passports and tickets for the *Lady Emerald* ship. He inspected them meticulously and when he was satisfied, he stacked them on the table. Bernadette reached for hers and slid it into her bag. Melvin noticed. "It's best to have all our documents in one place, babe."

"I'm an adult, Mel, I can hold my own passport."

A RADIO BROADCAST resounded as Melvin and Bernadette hauled their luggage into the lobby. The one-armed reception-ist grinned. "Oh, how the mighty have fallen. Your friend Nkrumah is finished." He turned up the transistor radio and General Kotoka's voice poured out:

"Fellow citizens of Ghana, I have come to inform you that the military, in cooperation with the Ghana Police, have taken over the government of Ghana today. The myth surrounding Nkrumah has been broken. Parlia-ment is dissolved and Kwame Nkrumah is dismissed from office."

Melvin couldn't believe what he'd just heard. He tried to keep his composure as he stacked their luggage inside the waiting taxi. The driver was an utter bundle of nerves. "I beg hurry up, curfew dey start six P.M.," he pleaded.

But Melvin wasn't listening. His mind had drifted to the one-armed receptionist, Kwesi, and the coup plotters who'd overthrown his friend Kwame Nkrumah. His rage crescen-doed, and he decided right there that he would seek ven-geance. So he poked his head into the passenger window. "I'll be right back, Bern."

Melvin disappeared into the guest house before the driver could protest. He marched to Kwesi's room and kicked the door off the hinges. His gaze darted around until it landed on Kwesi's beloved guitar. Melvin swung the guitar violently and it shattered on impact. Then he splashed kerosene from a lan-tern and struck a match. The room was soon engulfed in a ferocious fire that consumed everything it touched.

Melvin rushed outside, feeling his anger subside momen-tarily, relieved it was almost over. All they'd been through, fi-nally another country on the horizon. Then he stepped into the parking lot and a jolt of shock crippled him. His petrified eyes searched the empty lot where the taxi once stood. Berna-dette was gone, along with his shoulder bag where he carried all his money.

"Fuck! Fuck! Fuck!" Melvin screamed. Had Bernadette left him behind? Why would she do such a thing?

"Kwesi," he murmured. "Fuckin' Kwesi." He must have planned this with Bernadette the moment they decided to flee to yet another country. Melvin punched the air, cursing the day he crossed paths with Kwesi.

But Bernadette had planned this all by herself. She knew Melvin was easily distracted and all she needed was a sliver of a chance to break free from him. It didn't take much to con-vince the taxi driver to speed off. He was eager to complete the trip before the six P.M. curfew.

Melvin checked his watch anxiously. He had less than thirty minutes to get to the shipyard or risk being left behind in a country that was in free fall. He glanced back to see the Peacock Guest House consumed in a rapturous fire. Then he hurried outside the gate and flagged down the only tottering taxi on the main road. The old man behind the wheel was unaware of the looming curfew, so he blissfully opened the car door for the American pastor who was hiding a revolver in the small of his back.

KWESI HEARD THE wailing sirens as he approached the Peacock Guest House. A crowd had gathered outside to watch the mayhem. Flashing red lights from a fire engine brightened the smoldering structure. Kwesi, alarmed, pushed past the firemen dragging hoses. Then he heard the one-armed receptionist screaming, "Your American friend did this to me. I swear by the gods, he will pay for this."

Kwesi hurried to his room and stopped at the charred door frame. The remnants of his burnt guitar floated in the amalgam of ashes and embers. He dropped to his knees, paralyzed with shock. Melvin had done the unthinkable. He had destroyed his sacred guitar and taken Bernadette, most likely against her will. But beyond Bernadette, Kwesi now had an appetite for blinding revenge and it ached. He vowed that Melvin would pay, in blood if necessary.

IT WAS THE fourth armored car Agent Hughes spotted on the single-lane road.

"Something is wrong," he said to T, who was trembling at the wheel. His apprehension wasn't for himself per se. It was for the Renault Dauphine. He knew how much his brother loved that car and woe betide him if something dreadful happened to it.

"It must be a coup d'état," Agent Hughes finally said.

He turned on the radio and heard the Ghanaian national anthem abbreviated by a rebroadcast of General Kotoka's overthrow speech.

"Dammit." Agent Hughes slammed the dashboard angrily. "Today of all days, when I'm finally this close."

A fifth armored car zoomed by and Agent Hughes caught a glimpse of the soldiers armed with heavy-artillery weapons.

"I think we should turn around," he said timidly.

"I agree," T quavered.

Then suddenly an explosion throttled the vehicle, jolting T and Agent Hughes. They glanced to see a car tire burning fervently in the middle of the road. When the smoke cleared, General Kotoka's soldiers had already surrounded the Renault Dauphine.

THE SHIPYARD WAS crowded with frantic passengers when Kwesi arrived. Most were expats fleeing the country after news of President Nkrumah's overthrow spread like wildfire. A mammoth ship eclipsed the horizon, miniaturizing everything around it. The Liberian flag hoisted on the ship's stern cast a shadow on the bold sign: *THE LADY EMERALD.*

THAT WAS WHERE Kwesi searched ardently for Melvin and Bernadette. He had neither a plan nor an escape route. His only driving force was a burning desire for retribution. Kwesi joined the immigration queue, eyes peeled and alert. All he had to do was clear customs, and Melvin would be within reach. Kwesi handed his identification to the customs officer.

"Going to Monrovia?" the officer asked.

"Yes, Monrovia."

"Business or pleasure?"

"Pleasure."

"Anything to declare?"

"No, sah."

The officer stamped Kwesi's ticket and he paid with the same money Melvin had given him. Then suddenly an air-raid siren blared across the dock and a whirlwind of chaos ensued. Military trucks screeched to a halt and armed soldiers surrounded the ship. Kwesi was unperturbed by the ruckus. He climbed up to the ship's deck and a voice thundered from a bullhorn:

> *"Curfew has officially been instated. All passengers must disembark now. Have your identification ready for inspection. This ship has been grounded. Repeat. This ship has been grounded."*

Bernadette was hiding in the ladies' room when the melee broke out. The frightened passengers brushed past her and when she looked up, she saw Kwesi in the distance. He ran up to her, hugging her tightly.

"What are you doing here, Kwesi?" Bernadette asked, releasing herself from his embrace. "I'm fine, better even, on my own."

Kwesi nodded, feeling the sting of rejection. "I'm here for Melvin."

. . .

THE SHIPYARD WAS a chaotic scene when Melvin's taxi pulled up. He crept past the soldiers and scaled a forklift onto the cargo deck. He too was swarmed by the hysterical crowd fleeing the ship. He raised his gaze to see Kwesi and Bernadette talking on the deck. She carried her luggage in one hand and Melvin's shoulder bag in the other.

"I knew it," Melvin murmured, digging out his .38-caliber Ruger.

Melvin's eyes burned menacingly as he aimed the revolver at Kwesi. "You just won't go away, will you?"

Suddenly a petrified passenger pushed past Melvin, throwing him off balance. Kwesi looked beyond the passenger to see Melvin, gun in hand. Sensing this was his only chance, he pushed Bernadette out of the line of fire and leapt forward, wrestling Melvin to the ground. They both clutched the trigger of the gun, struggling to gain the upper hand. Bernadette floundered to her feet. She looked at the two men and knew that the right thing to do was to try to stop them, but she had a firm resolve to leave it all behind and start anew. So Bernadette turned swiftly to join the fleeing crowd as a loud bang echoed.

Kwesi and Melvin would play this moment back in their heads a thousand times and never understand how the gun went off, shattering Bernadette's slender frame. She crashed through the ship's railing and sank into the ocean. Both men screamed in horror, watching her disappear into the crashing waves. Melvin grabbed his shoulder bag and fled the deck, leaving Kwesi stunned. The last thing he saw was the crimson tide that swallowed Bernadette's lifeless body, before a soldier slammed his rifle butt into his face.

CHAPTER 18

K wesi heard the tottering sounds of a diesel engine when he gained consciousness. The blood that leaked from his forehead soaked his eyelids, obscuring his view. The swaying sensation of the armored truck and the saline smell of the ocean confirmed his assumption. They were still somewhere in Cape Coast. He wondered how long he had blacked out. The remnants of twilight were still visible across the horizon, so he figured he must have been out for at least an hour. The metal cuffs that bound his hands cut deeply into his flesh. He grimaced with each pothole the truck bumped over.

Then suddenly the armored truck came to a screeching halt. Kwesi peeked through the wire mesh window and saw a car burning ferociously. He gasped when he realized it was T's brother's Renault Dauphine. He had seen T driving it a few times with his arm cocked out the window to impress the ladies.

A clamoring sound followed, and then the heavy armored truck door flung open. Kwesi turned to see the silhouette of a white man, cuffed and badly beaten. They threw him in the back of the truck, and the bumpy ride resumed.

"Kwesi Kwayson?" the white man slurred, mouth full of blood.

"Yes? Do I know you?"

"No, but I know you. In fact, I've been looking for you."

The armored car struck a pothole and tossed the men against their metal cage. When they settled, the white man said, "My name is Hughes. Agent Hughes. I work for the FBI. I've been looking for Melvin Johnson and Bernadette Broussard."

It all made sense to Kwesi. Agent Hughes was the reason Melvin and Bernadette had been running. He looked back at the burning Renault Dauphine. "Was that T's car?"

Agent Hughes nodded. "They shot him and set the car on fire."

There was a brief silence, and then Kwesi quavered, "Bernadette is dead."

"What?"

"Yes," Kwesi said, eyes misty. "Melvin tried to shoot me. We fought over the gun, and it went off," he sniveled.

"Everything is fucked. Everything." Agent Hughes sighed.

THE ARMORED CAR drove past a spirited crowd in the middle of the road. They carried signs and photographs of General Kotoka, chanting in a loud chorus:

"Nkrumah is no more—Ghana is finally free."

"Did they really hate President Nkrumah that much?" Agent Hughes asked.

Kwesi was still wallowing in his pain. "I don't know. He won our independence and now we have turned against him."

His eyes were distant, as if having an epiphany. "I guess if an animal will bite you, it will be from your cloth."

· · ·

THE SUN WAS in its final throes when the armored truck pulled into a towering prison fort. It was built by the Danes in the sixteenth century when they too tried to cash in on the transatlantic slave trade. The large steel gates had been shipped from Copenhagen, and they swung menacingly as the armored truck pulled into the prison courtyard.

Agent Hughes and Kwesi disembarked and joined a queue of prisoners. A guard prodded Agent Hughes with the barrel of his gun. "Hey, obroni, join that line."

He ushered him to a queue for foreign nationals. They were mostly Russians, Chinese, other citizens of communist-leaning countries. The prison warden walked up to Agent Hughes, surprised to find an American in line. "You must have done something very stupid for your people to send you to us." He shoved a prison uniform into Agent Hughes's hands and marched him into a grim cell with Kwesi.

IT WAS AFTER midnight when Melvin finally made it to Ebo's house from the shipyard. He had waded through the low tide searching for Bernadette. He hoped that somehow she would have survived the shooting and swum ashore. But after several hours combing the area, he found no sign of her. Melvin waited until nightfall, then hiked atop a repugnant landfill, eluding a police checkpoint, until he made it to Ebo's house.

Exhausted from the trek, Melvin knocked on Ebo's door faintly. A fluorescent light above him attracted a flurry of insects. They dispersed when Ebo cracked the door slightly open. He was stunned to see Melvin, disheveled and dragging a suitcase.

"Pastor, you didn't leave yet?" he said as he ushered him

inside quickly. Ebo glanced to make sure no inquisitive neighbors were stretching their necks. When they were inside he asked, "What happened?"

"Your friend Kwesi took my wife and they left me."

"What?"

"They are gone."

"I suspected Kwesi liked your wife, sah, but I can't believe he would run away with her."

"I need a place to hide until the ship is allowed to leave."

"But Pastor—" Ebo started to say when Melvin cut him off.

"I'll pay you well." He unzipped his shoulder bag to show the rest of his money.

Ebo acquiesced, leading Melvin into a spare room where he kept boxes of forged documents. The walls were damp and moldy, but Melvin didn't care. He just needed a place to gather his thoughts. He opened the suitcase and realized that he had fled the shipyard with Bernadette's luggage instead of his own. Melvin grew misty-eyed as he unpacked Bernadette's neatly folded clothes. He saw her diary, bound together with Ma' Susan's letter and the totem of a mermaid.

Melvin hesitated, then flipped through Bernadette's diary. Each page conjured an agonizing pain. He thought he had read the most heartbreaking entries until he got to:

December 27th, 1965

Could it be? God, not now. Why now?
Me? Pregnant?
Ella seems so sure yet I can't tell Mel,
my fiancé, the father of my child.
It's all too much.

Melvin's heart sank. His guilt paralyzed him. He realized that he hadn't just killed his wife-to-be, he had killed his unborn child too. He punched the walls, grief-stricken. In that moment, Melvin regretted every decision he had made till that point. Beginning with that raining December night at Otto's Diner. He regretted fleeing America and regretted meeting Kwesi. Above all, he regretted coming to Ghana in search of his friend Nkrumah. The country he'd promised to rule in lieu of the British had collapsed, and the love of Melvin's life was dead. Melvin wiped the tears with the back of his hand. He decided that he would end it all right then. He reached for the .38-caliber Ruger, stuck it in his mouth, and mumbled, "God forgive me."

Then Melvin pulled the trigger but heard only a clicking sound. He pulled the trigger again and heard the same clicking sound. His hands trembled as he popped the revolver's chamber open to find that it was empty. It dawned on him that Corey had given him only one bullet.

"Fuck," he sighed.

THE FIRST NIGHT in the prison cell was hell. The humidity and mosquitoes were a deadly combination. Kwesi tossed and turned erratically. He wished he'd never gone to the shipyard in pursuit of Melvin. Bernadette would still be alive. Kwesi's mind flashed to the ship's deck and the crimson tide. His agonizing cries were only outdone by Agent Hughes's spasmodic heaving in the bunk bed below. His heart palpitations flared, and his medication was long gone. The next day another prisoner suddenly appeared in their cell. He reclined on the adjacent bunk bed languidly, exuding a deep meditative state. His gray beard ascribed a sagelike knowing. An ancient savant of sorts. When Agent Hughes asked the man his name, he simply replied, "Prof."

PROF WAS THE famed leader of the SSV. The mythical Shape-shifters Vanguard rumored to have rescued President Nkrumah from numerous assassination attempts. Agent Hughes remembered Officer Opoku's story about Prof and his elixir that transformed his soldiers into humanoid creatures. But he didn't believe a word of it. So as they sat in the cell with the strange man, neither Agent Hughes nor Kwesi bothered to ask Prof how he had suddenly appeared in their cell.

THE PRISON ROUTINE was the same every day. Breakfast at six A.M. Often the same miserable concoction of gari soakings or a sludgy substance that passed for porridge. Prisoners were allowed one hour of exercise before shower time. The chalky soap did little to lather the body, and the shower sprayed an odious discolored liquid. Dinner was served at eight P.M. prompt. The guards patrolled the dining hall, which was packed with former military personnel loyal to the now-deposed President Nkrumah.

All the foreign prisoners had been released on condition that their governments airlift them immediately. All but Agent Hughes and a Russian fella named Kuznetsov. His continued presence in the prison made Agent Hughes apprehensive. He surmised that Kuznetsov had been left behind to spy on him. That was certainly the Russian modus operandi, and Agent Hughes kept his distance.

. . .

KWESI ADJUSTED POORLY to life in prison. His guilt was an ever-present gnawing and he lamented to anyone who would listen. He was in the middle of his self-loathing diatribe when Prof interrupted him. "I know why you are here." It was the first full sentence Prof had uttered in the seven nights they had shared the cell with him.

"Why am I here?" Kwesi asked.

Prof rolled out of bed and sat up straight.

"You are here for me to guide you to your destiny."

"Destiny?" Kwesi asked, baffled.

Prof continued, "You were thrown overboard a ship. You were saved by Mami Wata, who gave you a guitar. You were ordered to play it on the eve of independence, not a day before and not a day after. You disobeyed. Your destiny is intertwined with our nation, Kwesi. When you bloom, it blooms, and when you burn, it burns. Only you can make this right."

Kwesi was awestruck. Who was this man? And how did he know all of this?

Agent Hughes just shrugged and threw the blanket over his head. "Mermaids and guitar voodoo, and I thought I had heard it all."

THAT NIGHT, PROF woke Kwesi up with a gentle tug.

"It's time," he whispered.

Kwesi, disoriented and still in the throes of slumber, couldn't tell if he was dreaming or awake. Agent Hughes was snoring in the bunk below when Prof led Kwesi to the center of the prison cell. His face was moonlit and his eyes gleamed, like those of a hawk. Prof pulled out three cowrie shells, shook them, and dropped them in a precise pattern. A large hole appeared in the concrete floor, and a grayish mist emanated from it. Prof stepped into the dark abyss and beckoned Kwesi to follow. They walked through the bowels of a giant mammal. A hard shell hovered above them and Kwesi guessed that they were inside a massive tortoise or crab. Then suddenly the creature hurled them out of its mouth and onto a dark savanna plain.

Prof stood up and wiped the slimy substance from his face.

"I never like this part," he said.

Kwesi was too stunned to utter a word. He just staggered behind Prof toward a baobab tree. They waited there, observing the bioluminescent fireflies that hovered all around them. Then a levitating canoe appeared on the horizon. Two soldiers paddled the thin air until they docked on the dry blades of grass.

"Successful mission, sah?" one of the soldiers asked, saluting Prof.

"Very successful."

The soldiers pulled Kwesi and Prof aboard the floating canoe and they began their journey into the ethereal night.

AGENT HUGHES'S EYES slowly adjusted to the light seeping through the iron bars. He heard the jingling of keys, followed by a loud squeaking sound. Then the cell door swung open. A soldier marched in and cuffed him to the metal frame of his bunk bed.

"He is ready, sah," the soldier said, as he marched out.

Agent Hughes looked up to see—Frank Dekker?

He had traded his long blond hair for a clean buzz fade. He wore a sharp black suit, a far contrast from his usual Hawaiian shirts and bell-bottom pants. He looked more like a banker than a vicious CIA operative. He sank into an adjacent chair and crossed his Italian moccasins on the bed.

"You son of a bitch! I should kill you," Agent Hughes barked.

Frank Dekker smiled and lit a cigarette. "Is this how you greet an old friend?"

"The Bureau will hear about this."

"The Bureau? What Bureau?" Frank Dekker took a long drag and exhaled. "You don't work for the Bureau anymore, Hughes. You were fired the minute you decided to skip your flight to Washington."

"Bullshit. I don't believe you."

"Well, believe what you wanna, old sport. My work here is done. I came to say goodbye. You should look me up if you're ever in Angola. I heard a government needs overthrowing and I happen to be unemployed."

Frank Dekker leapt up and doused his cigarette on Agent Hughes's pillow.

"Say, you wouldn't happen to know anything about that musician who escaped from your cell last night?"

"Fuck you," Agent Hughes spat in disgust.

"Yeah, I told the warden you wouldn't know, but I don't think he believes me. Good luck, Hughes." Frank Dekker strolled out of the jail, whistling the refrain to "Mami Wata Highlife."

CHAPTER 19

A whole week had passed and there was still no sign of Bernadette. Her body hadn't washed ashore and Melvin wondered if the police were still looking for her. He stayed indoors and avoided daylight. Consequently, Melvin began to develop a morbid case of cabin fever. He tried to kill himself again, but the dilapidated ceiling caved when he hanged himself with a bedsheet. After two failed attempts, Melvin decided he'd try to live, even if his days were eclipsed by impenetrable grief and regret.

THE *LADY EMERALD* was still under heavy military guard at the shipyard. Everyone waited for General Kotoka to reopen the country's borders and allow travel again. Melvin decided he would wait it out too. His temporary solace was Auntie Esi's palm wine that Ebo brought to him every morning. After a long day of drinking, Melvin borrowed Ebo's typewriter and decided to write Nkrumah one last letter.

```
Dear Nkrumah,
    This is Melvin Johnson, from Lincoln Univer-
sity. I'm sure you remember me. I saved your
```

life and you promised you would never forget it. I wonder why you have not bothered to answer any of my letters. I'm sure you received at least one of them before your unfortunate overthrow. At this point, I don't even care. I just want you to know a few things. I came to Ghana seeking asylum from you. I came with my fiancee, Bernadette, whom I loved. She is dead now. I'm not saying any of this is your fault, but you did not keep your word. I hear you have been granted asylum in Guinea. Well, it's not too late to do right by an old friend. I will be leaving for Liberia soon. If I make it out, I hope you can help me gain asylum in Guinea too. If not, I'll be a ghost by the time you read this letter.

Sincerely.
Melvin Johnson.

THE JOURNEY ABOARD the levitating canoe was otherworldly. Kwesi glanced at the endless blades of savanna grass that parted when the soldiers paddled. The atmosphere was still filled with ethereal fireflies. Prof sat meditatively on the floating stern, eyes closed and hands stretched. It was as if he was navigating telepathically.

Prof finally opened his eyes. "We are here."

He waved his hand and a sprawling military camp appeared. Kwesi was transfixed by the hundreds of soldiers jogging and practicing drills. They all stopped to salute Prof as they walked toward an encampment. A bright light glimmered from an army tent. When Kwesi parted the tarp, he saw his guitar. The same one the mermaid had given him. Kwesi's jaw dropped.

"Where did you get this?"

"We have our ways," Prof replied.

"But—it was destroyed in the fire," Kwesi said in utter bewilderment.

"Yes, we had a hard time putting it back together."

Kwesi instinctively reached for the guitar and Prof grabbed his shoulder. "Not yet."

Kwesi gazed at the spectacle outside. A military truck levitated toward him, leaving no tire marks on the wet mud. Kwesi looked up and saw a group of soldiers walking upside down. The skies receded in and out of darkness intermittently.

"What is this place?" he asked.

"This is the SSV. The Shapeshifters Vanguard."

"The SSV is real?"

"Yes. We are very real."

Kwesi was dumbfounded. He gazed at Prof, who snapped his fingers, and a fire ignited on his fingertip. He lit his pipe with the flame and continued. "We are the reason President Nkrumah survived all those assassination attempts. The Flagstaff House. The Kulungugu bombing. And many others you never heard about."

Prof took another drag from his pipe. "Now, our mission is to stage a countercoup, overthrow General Kotoka's government, and return Nkrumah to the presidency."

"So why am I here?"

"I thought you would never ask," Prof said, extinguishing his pipe. "Your guitar is powerful, Kwesi. It was supposed to protect our nation. That is why Mami Wata asked you to play it on the eve of independence. We have named our countercoup after your song 'Mami Wata Highlife.' My men requested to hear you perform it on the eve of our mission. It will be the protection we need."

Kwesi was overwhelmed by Prof's optimism. But if he was honest, he knew that his guitar brought misfortune wherever he went. Yes, he had scored a hit record with "Mami Wata Highlife," but his royalties had been stolen, Bernadette was dead, and President Nkrumah had been overthrown. How would this countercoup be any different? Prof could feel his hesitation. He pulled Kwesi close and whispered, "There is something in it for you."

"What's that?"

"Revenge! I'll show you where to find Melvin."

THAT NIGHT, THE soldiers drank Prof's elixir from a large cauldron. With each sip, a new spirit burst zestfully. A loud wailing guitar echoed around the camp. When the soldiers looked up, they saw Kwesi onstage, illuminated by a large bonfire. He fiddled his usual arpeggio and suddenly, a bright light engulfed the stage. The familiar chords of "Mami Wata Highlife" blared out of the speakers. The soldiers contorted to the melody. Then they began to transform into humanoid creatures. Hyenas, goats, ravens, roosters, wild boars, and lizards. Kwesi rubbed his eyes, still uncertain if this was a lucid dream. Then he struck the final chords of "Mami Wata Highlife" and the crescendo sent the soldiers into hysteria. Prof transformed into a humanoid hawk and fluttered onto the stage. He lifted Kwesi with his claws and yelled: "Operation Mami Wata—activated."

A mélange of growls, chirps, quacks, shrieks, and roars reverberated across the camp.

THEY CALLED IT the red room for two reasons. The first was because of the large red light that brightened the torture chamber. The second was because of the copious amounts of blood the prison janitors had to mop up after each torture session. Agent Hughes hung upside down on a meat hook, gazing at the pool of blood that dripped from his torso and gathered on the cold concrete floor.

"How did Kwesi escape?" the guard yelled, for what felt like the hundredth time.

Agent Hughes tried to speak, but the rush of blood to his head made it impossible. His body was failing, and he could tell. He felt the splash of cold water on his face. It both revived him and sent him into shock. The guard pulled a lever and Agent Hughes came crashing down.

This was the second night he had visited the red room, and no matter how much they beat and tortured him, Agent Hughes had no idea how Kwesi had vanished without a trace. When he described Prof and suggested that he might have helped Kwesi escape, the guards laughed hysterically. They had arrested no one by that name or description.

THE BROKEN MIRROR in the jail cell had been defaced by previous inmates. When Agent Hughes wiped his blood-soaked eyes, he only saw a fraction of himself. His stubby beard, filthy and unkempt, attracted a flurry of flies. In that moment, he remembered his father's famous words, "You can't trust a country that will sell out its own people for profit." Ghana was indeed profitable, and Agent Hughes had stuck his nose where it didn't belong. In that moment, he wished he'd never gotten on that plane to Ghana in pursuit of Melvin and Bernadette.

THE EVENING DRAB had descended on the prison courtyard when Agent Hughes joined the other inmates. They relished the time spent outside their damp, mildewed cells. Agent Hughes was too sore to walk, so he sat quietly on a bench. The only Russian fella left in the prison walked up to him and offered a cigarette.

"Privet," he said.

Agent Hughes's eyes darted around as he cupped the cigarette, igniting it with a match.

"I'm Kuznetsov," the Russian fella said.

"Hughes," Agent Hughes replied, exhaling a thick puff of smoke.

"Why they put you here?" Kuznetsov asked.

"I was gonna ask you the same thing." Agent Hughes shrugged.

"I disobey order. You?"

"Same."

Kuznetsov stroked his thick Stalin-esque mustache. "I have secret. Kuznetsov not my name. Petrov my real name. You?"

"Hughes is my real name, well, the name I gave to myself. Pawlowski is my family name."

"Pawlowski? Polish?"

"Yes." Agent Hughes nodded.

"Look, I see what they do to you in red room. Very bad. I

leave to Russia tomorrow. My government negotiate for me. I can help you if you like to be release."

Agent Hughes extinguished the cigarette on the concrete, then whispered, "You can help me get out of here?"

"If you like, my government do this sometimes."

Agent Hughes thought about the cold cell, the red room, and the torture that awaited him the next day. Then he asked, "What do you need from me?"

"Nothing. We already have everything. You just decide what country you go to, and we make passport. I don't suggest America." Kuznetsov smirked.

THAT EVENING, AGENT Hughes paced his empty cell pensively. He was seriously considering Kuznetsov's offer. Then he wondered, why the generosity? Was it a trap? Did they hope to turn him into an asset? He knew the consequences of collaborating with the enemy. But his heart palpitations had gotten worse, and he dreaded the torture chamber. This was a risk worth taking.

Agent Hughes decided on Poland, because he wished to see his father again. Perhaps they would visit his ancestral home of Częstochowa, or meet his extended family in Bydgoszcz. Agent Hughes knew there was no turning back from this decision. So he was resolute when he shook hands with Kuznetsov at dinner and the deal was done.

EBO WAS UPBEAT when he burst into Melvin's room that morning.

"Hallelujah," he screamed, waving a copy of the *Daily*

Graphic. Melvin's eyes lit up when he saw the bold headline: *GHANA'S BORDERS OPEN TOMORROW.*

"Finally!" Melvin sighed.

"Yes, finally," Ebo echoed. He had done his best to accommodate his moody American guest, whose suicidal tendencies unsettled Ebo. So he was just as ecstatic as Melvin about the good news. He bought a pot of palm wine from Auntie Esi, and they drank to their hearts' content. Ebo turned on the transistor radio to celebrate. Then suddenly the familiar chords of "Mami Wata Highlife" filled the room. Ebo knew this was a trigger for Melvin, whose fiancée he thought Kwesi had eloped with. A sudden gloom descended on Melvin. Ebo rushed to turn off the radio, and then Prof's voice interrupted the song:

> *"Fellow Ghanaians. Do not panic. This is the SSV here to announce that Operation Mami Wata is in effect. General Kotoka is dead. I repeat, General Kotoka is dead. His illegal government that overthrew Kwame Nkrumah is on the brink of defeat. We advise you to stay indoors for your safety and await further instructions. Long live the SSV. Long live President Nkrumah. Long live Ghana."*

"Goddammit!" Melvin yelled. "Another fuckin' coup d'état?"

PROF AND HIS SSV army had launched their countercoup earlier that morning. It began at approximately eight A.M. when loud shrieks, grunts, and hoots resounded around the capital city. A group of humanoid creatures stormed the Ghana Broadcasting Corporation in broad daylight. Their leader, Prof, instructed the radio engineers to play "Mami Wata Highlife," their code song used to alert the SSV soldiers en route to ambush General Kotoka.

He was leaving the airport when a rocket-propelled grenade torpedoed his caravan. Heavy artillery fire was exchanged between the SSV soldiers and General Kotoka's guards. When the smoke cleared, General Kotoka lay dead on the tarmac.

The SSV soldiers thought they had succeeded in overthrowing General Kotoka's government, but they were soon overwhelmed by an aerial assault. The soldiers drank their elixirs and fled the airport. When Prof got the news, his heart sank. All their efforts had been for naught. Yes, the SSV had succeeded in killing General Kotoka, but his government survived, and Operation Mami Wata had failed.

CHAPTER 20

Kwesi had been walking through an arid pasture with no respite. The SSV camp had disappeared, leaving dry blades of savanna grass that brushed against his arms as he waded toward the baobab tree. Strangely, the tree seemed farther away with each step he took. It had been this way for hours and the sun had neither risen nor set. Just as he capitulated to the humidity, Kwesi saw a three-legged dog hobbling toward him. It stopped, stared briefly, and turned around. Kwesi followed the dog until he arrived at a bungalow floating in the air above a hill. A solitary light illuminated the structure and Kwesi glanced to see an old woman hunched over a daguerreotype camera. A black cloak covered her head and she held out a flashbulb that burst into shimmering sparks. The old woman unfurled the cloak and smiled.

"You must be Kwesi."

Kwesi nodded, and then he realized that the old woman was blind. She tapped her cane around and led Kwesi toward the floating bungalow. The three-legged dog stayed on the porch, keeping guard.

"Where am I?" Kwesi asked, bewildered.

"You are on the path traveled only by the chosen."

"Do you know Prof?"

"Prof is my son."

"Is he all right?"

"I take it you haven't heard the news."

The blind old woman fixed Kwesi a potion and told him about the failed countercoup and General Kotoka's death.

"What about Prof?" Kwesi inquired nervously.

"Nobody knows where he is. But I know my son. He will return home when he is ready."

Kwesi sighed deeply, his eyes catching the still portraits hanging neatly on the wall.

"You took these?" Kwesi asked, gazing at the black-and-white photos of Nkrumah. Each frame captured the rise of the now-deposed president.

"I was Nkrumah's personal photographer. Do you recognize anything familiar?"

Kwesi saw himself playing his guitar in the background of President Nkrumah dancing with Queen Elizabeth.

"You were there?" he asked, awestruck.

"I was there from the beginning until the end. I watched Nkrumah build up a mighty nation and watched him descend into paranoia. Jailing his opponents to stop them from undermining his vision. Building a dam he couldn't afford. Declaring himself president for life."

Kwesi started to feel drowsy. His eyelids got heavier, burdened by the weight of his plight. The blind old woman walked up to him. "You can spend the night here. Tomorrow, I will show you the way home."

. . .

THAT NIGHT, KWESI, Agent Hughes, and Melvin all slept in different worlds, but with the same raison d'être. Kwesi snored in the blind old woman's bungalow, floating in a realm that was neither reality nor mirage. Agent Hughes tossed and turned in the cold prison cell, with armed guards patrolling the hallways. And Melvin dozed in Ebo's squalid storeroom, with his ticket for the *Lady Emerald* under his pillow. When the first light stretched across the morning sky, each man awoke to a singular fate that was intertwined from the beginning.

A KETTLE WHISTLED loudly as Kwesi walked into the kitchen. The room was bathed in sunlight, casting a shadow on the SSV banner that hung above a photo of Prof. He looked younger and blithesome, with the same sagacious air, radiating a deep knowing.

The blind old woman's voice seeped from the back room. "Come in, Kwesi."

Kwesi opened the door gently and entered the den. It had a red fluorescent tube that hung above a cluster of still cameras. The blind old woman had just finished running a photograph through a chemical bath. She wiped her hands on her apron. "Here are the pictures from your camera."

Kwesi stared at his Pentax in astonishment.

"How did my camera get here?"

The blind old woman smiled. "We have our ways."

Kwesi glanced to see a slew of photographs hanging on a thin wire. They were the pictures he had taken on their journey, mostly of Bernadette. The most beautiful of all was the photograph of her standing next to the cannons at Elmina

Castle. A deep sadness overcame Kwesi. The blind old woman consoled him. "I know you are hurting, my son, I can sense a great loss." She unfurled an SSV blanket and handed Kwesi a double-barreled shotgun. "But I must warn you, he who embarks on a path of revenge must dig two graves."

Kwesi had reached the bitter end. Bernadette was dead, and he was partly to blame. He had lost his guitar, the one thing that seemed to make him invincible, or so he thought. Revenge was the only thing worth living for now. Kwesi slung the shotgun over his shoulder and turned to the blind old woman.

"Thank you for your help. I hope Prof finds his way home soon."

She nodded and served Kwesi an elixir. "Behind the house is a river that runs backward," she said. "Drink this when you see your own reflection, and then you will see Melvin. You are now one and the same."

THE *LADY EMERALD* was finally cleared to depart for Liberia. Even after General Kotoka's assassination, the new military government decided it was necessary to open the country's borders. The news excited Melvin; he was finally getting out of this hellhole. He didn't know what awaited him in Liberia, but it couldn't be worse than what he had experienced in Ghana. Melvin packed his few belongings and realized that he was almost out of money. His shoulder bag that contained his entire life savings was depleted. Ebo had gone in search of a taxi and Melvin wondered where he had kept the money he'd paid him for the passports. He ransacked Ebo's house and after exhausting every possible crevice, he collapsed into the couch and the plastic cover squeaked. Then it suddenly dawned on Melvin. He grabbed a kitchen knife and slashed the cushion until he saw the secret compartment in the couch. Melvin counted almost five thousand dollars. He was surprised to find a brand-new Beretta pistol, stashed among the stolen passports. Melvin checked the magazine chamber and it was fully loaded. He smirked and hurried out of Ebo's house.

AGENT HUGHES HAD his doubts until the black GAZ Chaika pulled into the prison yard. The guard unshackled his cuffs and marched him through the courtyard. He turned to see the prison gate slam shut behind him. It was really happening, he thought.

"Zdravstvuyte," the heavyset driver said, tipping his hat.

Agent Hughes caught his own reflection in the passenger window. His suit hung shabbily over his lean frame, bruised and dowdy. He had shaved with a blunt razor that morning and it scarred his face. The driver continued in a thick Russian accent, "Pozhaluysta. Get in. We are late."

Agent Hughes quickly slid into the back seat of the GAZ and exhaled deeply. The driver handed him an envelope and whispered, "Compliments of Kuznetsov."

Agent Hughes emptied the contents to find a LOT Polish Airlines ticket and a burgundy passport with the words *POLSKA PASZPORT.*

He flipped to the information page and gazed at his photograph. It was the same one from his American passport, but aged to match the new Polish aesthetic. The name below the photo was *Mikhail Pawlowski.* Agent Hughes smiled. No one had called him Mikhail in over ten years, and it made him think about his father. He never imagined that he would miss Leo Pawlowski, but the thought of reuniting filled him with great joy. As the GAZ Chaika drove down the Cape Coast road, Agent Hughes glanced back to see the prison for the last time. He definitely wouldn't miss it.

THE DRIVE WAS relatively comfortable, except for the chastushka Russian folk music that blared out of the speakers, completely out of place in the grueling Ghanaian heat. The driver maneuvered through the Cape Coast traffic, with bustling street vendors hawking their goods at every roundabout. Not much had changed since Nkrumah's overthrow, Agent Hughes reckoned. The streets were still crowded and the traffic was dense. All in all, Ghana was still the same Ghana: hot, humid, and arduous.

As they waited in the traffic, Agent Hughes glanced to see a group of soldiers huddled around a fire pit. They dumped boxes of vinyl records, splashed kerosene, and struck a match, engulfing the albums in flames. The Russian driver adjusted the rearview mirror, catching Agent Hughes's reflection. "They banned that 'Mami Wata' song after the SSV coup. So the army find all copies and burn. Illegal to own that album now." Agent Hughes shook his head in disbelief. He felt a deep sympathy for Kwesi. The once-beloved musician had now become a pariah in his own country. He remembered Kwesi's words on that fateful night they rode in the armored truck to the prison: *If an animal will bite you, it will be from your cloth.*

AFTER FIVE NERVOUS hours, the GAZ Chaika pulled into the airport parking lot. It all felt like déjà vu to Agent Hughes. It was at this same airport that he had made the terrible decision to call T. Not this time. Getting out of Ghana was his only goal now.

"Do svidaniya," the driver said, as he shook Agent Hughes's hand with short stubby fingers. "Our agent meet you at Warsaw Airport. He have picture. Good luck."

AGENT HUGHES THANKED him and walked through the sliding doors of the departure lounge, toward the LOT Polish desk. A blond ticket agent wearing a red beret checked his passport. "Cześć, Mr. Pawlowski. Any bags, sir?"

Agent Hughes shook his head.

"Okay, you are all set." The lady handed him his passport and a boarding pass.

Agent Hughes checked his watch. It was ten minutes to departure. All he could think about was reconciling with his father and building a new life in Poland. The airport intercom rattled with an announcement for the LOT Polish flight to Warsaw.

That was when Agent Hughes felt the paralyzing jolt through his chest. He reached in his suit pocket for his pills, but they were long gone. The palpitations worsened and Agent Hughes collapsed in his seat. The boarding had begun and passengers squeezed past him to join the queue. All he had to do was get up, walk to the gate, and he would be free. But his legs wouldn't move. "Dammit," Agent Hughes cried to himself. "Not now. Not here. Get up."

But he couldn't move a muscle. Tears flooded his eyes as he watched the other passengers board the flight. He tried to lift his hand for help, but he couldn't. Then he crashed violently to the floor. The last thing Agent Hughes saw was the high heels of the ticket agent running toward him.

KWESI HAD NO idea how he'd arrived at the shipyard. He vaguely remembered the blind old woman and the river that ran backward. The remnants of the elixir left an awful taste in his mouth. Then he felt a poke in his trousers and dug out the double-barreled shotgun. Yes, he remembered why he was at the shipyard now. The *Lady Emerald* was overwhelmed with passengers scrambling to flee Ghana, and Kwesi combed through the crowd with one target in mind: Melvin. He kept his hands on the trigger of the shotgun; he wouldn't be caught off guard this time. After a thorough search, Kwesi wagered that Melvin was at the canoe docks, knowing he wouldn't be able to resist the allure of fresh palm wine.

He was right. Melvin had been waiting to board the ship when he felt a deep melancholy. He was back to the same place where Bernadette was killed, and the guilt was too much to bear. So he decided he'd get a drink before the *Lady Emerald* departed.

Melvin was sitting leisurely aboard a floating canoe, sipping a calabash of palm wine, when he spotted Kwesi walking toward the dock. Melvin ducked, and a malevolent feeling overcame him. He too wanted revenge for Kwesi's part in Bernadette's death. He aimed Ebo's Beretta pistol and fired. The blast jolted the fishermen and they scurried away. The bullet missed Kwesi by inches, and he slid behind the billowing flags that hung from the canoe stern.

Melvin wrested control of the canoe outboard motor and

steered it toward the ocean. Kwesi, knowing it was now or never, jumped into a vacant canoe and maneuvered swiftly behind Melvin. The high-speed boat chase sent onlookers rushing to the docks. Kwesi spun and fired at Melvin, grazing his shoulder. The splash of blood and sharp pain distracted him. He lost control of the canoe and crashed into a wave that capsized it. Kwesi tried to maneuver around the wreckage, but it was too late. Both canoes splintered into bits, plunging Melvin and Kwesi into the sea. Neither man could swim, and they kicked ferociously, only exacerbating their imminent descent into the deep dark ocean. As they drowned, a bright pulsating glow blinded them. Then suddenly Bernadette appeared, in the form of a mermaid, silhouetted by a resplendent halo. A flurry of flowers bloomed all around her, each petal illuminating the reefs below. Her hair was adorned with a string of pearls that glistened when she hovered above Melvin and Kwesi. Both men's arms flailed frantically, desperately reaching out to her while fighting the weight of the ocean. Bernadette's eyes lit afire; only able to save one man, she swam ferociously.

EPILOGUE

Guinea Conakry, 1967

The large balcony of Villa Syli sat adjacent to the Gulf of Guinea, emitting a saline breeze. A slight drizzle whistled through the leaves, obscuring the colonial building in the pre-dawn light. That was where the former president stood anxiously, waiting for his trusted aide-de-camp, Camara. He had become his loyal confidant, and they remained inseparable since he arrived in Guinea, an arrival that was both spontaneous and disorienting for the former president. He'd never imagined a coup d'état would topple his government. Not after all he had done to bring his people independence. Twelve months of living in exile had taught him that anything was possible, and yet he couldn't accept the reality of his ouster.

THE FORMER PRESIDENT checked his watch again and gazed into the horizon, hoping to see the flickering lights of Camara's boat. The same boat he used on clandestine missions when he suspected the roads leading to Villa Syli were unsafe. Had Camara abandoned him too? That wouldn't be surprising. The former president had come to expect this after his own Ghanaian delegation defected en masse, the morning after his overthrow.

The only person who remained loyal was the president of Guinea, Sékou Touré. He offered him asylum and refused to acknowledge the government of General Kotoka. This was President Touré's way of thanking him for his generous gift of ten million dollars to the Guinean people, after they gained independence from France. The former president had chosen Guinea as temporary refuge for this exact reason. He needed the comfort of a country that still revered him. The twenty-one-gun salute that echoed on the tarmac when his plane touched down in Conakry was proof. The former president glanced out the window, turned to his delegation, and said, "We may not be home, but we are home."

A presidential motorcade drove him and his entourage to Villa Syli, which was to be their temporary residence. Upon arrival at the villa gates, thousands of Guinean citizens flanked the limousine, clamoring to welcome the now-deposed president.

THAT NIGHT, THE former president barely got a wink of sleep. He tossed and turned anxiously, and then he leapt out of bed and wandered through the villa, which once housed the famed French colonial governor, René Barthes. The high ceilings, large windows, and ornate fixtures reminded him of the Flagstaff House in Accra, the nexus of his power from which he once ruled Ghana. His anger and frustration turned to melancholy and despair. How did he end up here? What would become of his people now that he wasn't there to guide them?

The former president walked toward the balcony and heard the chirping of crickets, punctuated by the sound of waves lapping against the stone walls of Villa Syli. He broke down and sobbed quietly. "All my toil was for naught," he repeated to himself. The struggle for independence had been undermined by his own people. He knew that foreign agitators and imperialists had set the plan in motion, but his own people willingly dropped the guillotine.

When the former president woke the next morning, his entire delegation had disappeared. They absconded with the little money he had and slipped across the Guinean border. This was the final nail in his coffin. He was truly alone now, exiled in a foreign country, with no way to reclaim his presidency.

That was when Camara, a young Guinean graduate, was assigned to be his translator and secretary. Besides being a skilled typist, Camara spoke French, English, and Spanish fluently, which made him a key asset. He quickly rose to be the former president's aide-de-camp, setting up a headquarters in Villa Syli. It consisted of an administrative office and a radio broadcasting center. Inspired by Camara's work, the former president wasted no time setting a plan in motion. He paced back and forth in the corridors of Villa Syli, reciting a proclamation he intended to broadcast to the people of Ghana. Camara's typewriter reverberated in the small office as he struck the keys fervently, only pausing to read back the words.

When the former president was finally satisfied with the proclamation, he dipped his presidential pen in ink, a ritual he had become used to when he ruled Ghana by decree, and scribbled his signature in cursive. After a short rehearsal, Camara turned on the radio transmitter and said, "Your people are ready for you, Monsieur le Président." The former president cleared his throat, leaned into the microphone, and began with his favorite line, "My fellow Ghanaian revolution-aries."

THE BROADCAST LASTED only five minutes, but its effects were felt globally. The American embassy in Guinea immediately scrambled the radio signal at Villa Syli. Then they sabotaged communication cables to divert future transmissions. General Kotoka's government also decreed that it was a crime for Ghanaian citizens to listen to the former president. His books were banned and any remaining statues that had been erected in his honor were torn down.

UNDETERRED BY THE backlash, the former president began clandestine efforts to foment a countercoup, the most ambitious of which was code-named Operation Mami Wata. On the day of the countercoup, the former president was so certain that he would snatch victory from the jaws of defeat that he ordered Camara to pack all his belongings and prepare to vacate Villa Syli. He dressed up in his presidential smock, the one he wore on Independence Day, and wrote a triumphant speech. He even arranged to have President Touré's plane fly him to Ghana that night. Everyone in Guinea held their breath as the former president waited for a phone call confirming that General Kotoka's government had fallen. But as the minutes turned to hours, and the hours turned to days, and the days turned to weeks, it was clear that Operation Mami Wata had failed.

THE FORMER PRESIDENT slipped into a deep depression after the failed countercoup. He wandered aimlessly through Villa Syli, often mumbling incoherently to himself. He lost all appetite and barely touched the food Camara served him. He stopped reading the newspapers from Ghana and declined all visitors. To make things worse, a cable intercepted by Guinean intelligence exposed a plot to poison him at Villa Syli. This news exacerbated his paranoia, and he descended into hermitage. No one saw him in public for weeks, and even the Cuban doctor sent by his old friend Fidel Castro was barred from seeing him. His only solace during the months of ill health was Camara. Every night, Camara read his favorite book, Alexandre Dumas's *The Count of Monte Cristo*. He would drift in and out of consciousness as Camara's baritone voice filled the bedroom.

"All human wisdom is contained in these two words—Wait and Hope." He'd repeat Alexandre Dumas's famous words, his body consumed by a feverish bonfire. The rhythm of his breathing was Camara's only sign that the former president had drifted into a deep slumber. He would mark the page with his thumb and blow out the lamp that sat on the wooden table next to a miniature flag of Ghana.

As THE MONTHS wore on and the mystical aura that surrounded the former president began to fade, he decided that he would write a book. He surmised that it would also offer him temporary respite from his current quandary. So he began scribbling a draft for a book titled *How to Destroy Neo-Colonization*, which he later changed to *The Handbook of Revolutionary Warfare*.

Camara was thrilled to see the former president upbeat again. They worked long hours, beginning at dawn and continuing until midnight on most days. Sometimes President Touré visited Villa Syli and the former president eagerly shared new drafts of his book. Their conversations often drifted into the topic of reclaiming the presidency of Ghana. President Touré encouraged him to invade his own country with Guinea's army, but the former president objected vehemently.

"Not a single drop of blood will be spilled in my quest to save my people," he said, much to President Touré's disappointment.

This was the unwavering resolve that kept him alive as the months went by and soon the first anniversary of his overthrow was upon him. The former president planned to make another broadcast to Ghana, encouraging his people to resist their new government and prepare for his return. He spent several hours writing a proclamation that night and planned to have Camara type it in the morning. But when he woke up, Camara was gone, leaving a solitary guard at the main gate of Villa Syli.

A DESPERATE AIR hung above the former president as he checked his watch again. The fluttering leaves had absorbed the morning dew and there was still no sign of Camara. "It's all over now, everyone has abandoned me," he sighed, wiping a tear with the back of his hand. Just as he turned toward the villa doors, the sounds of an outboard motor echoed across the distant ocean. "Camara!" he yelled. "Thank God!"

CAMARA DOCKED THE boat and hurried toward the back entrance of Villa Syli, carrying a large wooden box on his broad shoulders. "Excusez-moi, Monsieur le Président," Camara said, struggling to catch his breath. "I'm sorry to be late. Post office called that you have package. They are afraid the Americans will sabotage, so I have to go quickly. You were sleeping and I don't want to bother you, sir."

"No problem," the former president replied. "You are the only one left in this world I can trust, Camara. Thank you."

Camara smiled, relishing the compliment of his hero. He swung a crowbar at the fragile box and it cracked open, spilling its contents. The former president's eyes widened, scanning the stacks of letters bound neatly with thread. Unbeknownst to him, a loyal supporter at the Ghana Post Office had taken it upon herself to hold all letters addressed to the former president. She smuggled them onto a freight ship heading to Guinea along with a detailed log of foreign agents who received mail at the post office.

"This is why you can never kill the revolution," the former president said to Camara, as they sorted through hundreds of letters. They organized them by dates, country stamps, and diplomatic seals. Then suddenly the former president froze. He stared at an envelope with the return address:

Melvin Johnson
PO Box 45
Cape Coast, Ghana

The former president quickly tore open the envelope and read Melvin's letter. His eyes grew misty and his hands trembled. "Who is it from, sir?" Camara asked. The former president's gaze was fixed on what seemed to be a pulsating glow in the distant ocean. There was a brief silence, and then he replied, "A ghost."

ACKNOWLEDGMENTS

Long before I had a novel, I had the title: *The Scent of Burnt Flowers*. I would often revisit it with hopes of conjuring something equally poetic. Perhaps a screenplay for a movie, or a musical composition for my next album. It wasn't until the global pandemic struck that the idea for a book crystallized. I found myself alone, quarantined in a world that had ground to a halt. The solitude forced me to ponder my earliest memories of growing up in Ghana, often eavesdropping on conversations between my parents and their friends. Their banter usually meandered through various topics: the state of the country, the price of petrol, government corruption, and, alas, "the good old days." One man's name was evoked whenever "the good old days" were discussed: Ghana's former president Osagyefo Dr. Kwame Nkrumah. I would hover around the adults, pretending to gather empty beer bottles that sat idly on the center table, and listen to anecdotes about this legendary, mythical figure, the man who snatched Ghana from the hands of the mighty British empire. Those stories of Nkrumah in my living room were far more spectacular than what my elementary teachers taught us in school. Their history was unimaginative and dry. On the other hand, my parents' friends' recollection of the events was magical and otherworldly. Thinking back, that is where the idea for this book was born. I've always wanted to write about Ghana's postcolonial hero, President Nkrumah. His rise to power and fall from grace. But I never wanted to write the unimaginative version. Deep down, I've always been intrigued by the human capacity to ascribe extraordinary attributes to people and events. Our insatiable need to embellish and imbue hyperbole to the mundane and banal. This is the lens through which I wanted to explore Ghana's history, just like my parents and their friends huddled around empty beer bottles. I am greatly indebted to Gabriel Mena and Natalia Williams, my circle with whom I share every crazy idea. They helped me shape this book into what it is today. The feedback of my agents, Anthony Mattero and Dan Rabinow, was essential in elevating this book. The ultimate arrival of my editor, Chelcee Johns, was what carried me across the finish line. Her firm guiding hand and velvet touch ensured that I would not take the path of least resistance.

That said, this book is a work of fiction. Some events are born out of reality but have been grossly dramatized for fictional effect. The timelines are nonlinear and cyclical, a homage to my grandmother's nocturnal stories by the fireside. Her ability to combine mythical creatures and real-life events is the bedrock of this book. The worlds we traverse are expansive and connect the African continent with the diaspora. The inspiration of the civil rights movement in America and independence movement in Africa is central to this story. I honor the countless African Americans who relocated to Ghana and other African countries, fleeing oppression and discrimination.

I mention the *Daily Graphic* a number of times in this book. Although the headlines are fictional, the newspaper is very real and has been a symbol of the free press in Ghana for decades. Finally, I owe a great debt of gratitude to the pioneers of highlife music, which is the lifeblood of this book. Legends like Ebo Taylor, C. K. Mann, Koo Nimo, and Nana Ampadu were my sonic inspiration. Thanks to all my friends and family members whom I pestered to read draft after draft. I am truly grateful to you all.

ABOUT THE AUTHOR

BLITZ BAZAWULE is a multidisciplinary artist born in Ghana. His feature directorial debut, *The Burial of Kojo*, premiered on Netflix via ARRAY Releasing. He co-directed Beyoncé's *Black Is King*, which earned him a Grammy nomination. Bazawule is set to direct the feature musical adaptation of *The Color Purple* for Warner Bros. His artwork has been featured at the Whitney Biennial. He is also a TED senior fellow and a Guggenheim fellow.

blitzbazawule.com
Facebook.com/BlitzAmbassador
Twitter: @BlitzAmbassador
Instagram: @blitzambassador

ABOUT THE TYPE

This book was set in Sabon, a typeface designed by the well-known German typographer Jan Tschichold (1902–74). Sabon's design is based upon the original letter forms of sixteenth-century French type designer Claude Garamond and was created specifically to be used for three sources: foundry type for hand composition, Linotype, and Monotype. Tschichold named his typeface for the famous Frankfurt typefounder Jacques Sabon (c. 1520–80).